"You make me out to be a bluebeard."

His hard gaze trapped her.

"He was a piker compared to you," she retorted. "How many of us do you want to dangle on a string? Sheila, Rhonda, me, and who knows who else."

"Try the entire population of Phoenix," he suggested, allowing his own anger to show. "Maybe we'll throw in New York and London too!"

Her green eyes blazed. "I wouldn't be surprised."

Another crack of thunder sounded as if it were in the room with them, making Brittany jump. And then his arms went around her and his lips crushed hers, bruising her mouth with a powerful urgency, kissing her resolve away, kissing her anger to shreds, and reducing her to a woman with unquenched desire.

"There," he said, finally lifting his mouth from hers, "that's from Bluebeard. That's what you're turning away." He pushed her from him and stalked out, slamming the door behind him.

Dear Reader:

After more than one year of publication, SECOND CHANCE AT LOVE has a lot to celebrate. Not only has it become firmly established as a major line of paperback romances, but response from our readers also continues to be warm and enthusiastic. Your letters keep pouring in—and we love receiving them. We're getting to know you—your likes and dislikes—and want to assure you that your contribution does make a difference.

As we work hard to offer you better and better SECOND CHANCE AT LOVE romances, we're especially gratified to hear that you, the reader, are rating us higher and higher. After all, our success depends on *you*. We're pleased that you enjoy our books and that you appreciate the extra effort our writers and staff put into them. Thanks for spreading the good word about SECOND CHANCE AT LOVE and for giving us your loyal support. Please keep your suggestions and comments coming!

With warm wishes,

Ellen Edwards

Ellen Edwards
SECOND CHANCE AT LOVE
The Berkley/Jove Publishing Group
200 Madison Avenue
New York, NY 10016

Second Chance at Love™

SMOLDERING EMBERS
MARIE CHARLES

A

**SECOND CHANCE AT LOVE
BOOK**

To Pat Teal with undying gratitude
for having shown me the way

SMOLDERING EMBERS

Copyright © 1982 by Marie Charles

Distributed by Berkley/Jove

First edition published August 1982

First printing

"Second Chance at Love" and the butterfly emblem are trademarks belonging to Jove Publications, Inc.

Printed in the United States of America

Second Chance at Love books are published by
The Berkley/Jove Publishing Group
200 Madison Avenue, New York, NY 10016

chapter

1

THE BALD-HEADED MAN behind the desk at the employment agency raised his eyebrows at the application in his hand and glared at Brittany Sinclair over the top of his reading glasses. He was just like all the others, she thought, except that he didn't look kind. Instead, he looked annoyed because she was taking up his time. Well, she was sorry she didn't have a Ph. D. for him, but she wouldn't have needed him then.

A few weeks ago she would never have dreamed she'd be in this position, searching for a job and having no basic skills. But then she had been Rev. Sinclair's wife, living in a small, comfortable house with a small, comfortable man. The car crash had changed all that. Now, with expressions of sympathy still ringing in her ears, Brittany found herself widowed, homeless, and with very little to her name except an old car, her history books on western Indian tribes, and a few clothes. A sorry state for any twenty-four-year-old woman. But she was determined to get her life back in order.

Her bright green eyes watched the employment agent as he put the form down and ran a finger along the first line on the second page.

"No education," he read aloud. He glanced up at Brittany almost accusingly.

"Three courses shy of an English degree," she corrected with just a hint of indignation. She didn't like the man's condescending manner. She had almost finished a degree last spring—and then Jonathan had demanded more of her time, and the final courses had been put off "until next semester," which never came.

"You might as well be thirty courses shy," he told her. "All they care about," he informed her, tapping the large box of index cards on his desk that bore the names of potential employers and their present requirements, "is the end result. Degrees are always good to have, no matter what you're doing." Brittany wondered if the plaques hanging on the wall behind him testifying to several different degrees were genuine or just for show. "No job experience," she heard him say.

"I worked for my husband," she told him. And it was as hard a job as any she might have received pay for, she added silently. Harder, probably. The hours had been endless.

"And he is . . . ?"

"Was," she corrected. "A minister."

"Very little calling for minister's wives these days," he said sarcastically. "Can you type?" There was a note of exasperation in his voice.

"A little."

"Then we won't ask you about shorthand, will we?"

She found herself getting angry. Words came to her lips before she could get them under control. "Mr. Simmons," she said, glancing at the nameplate to make sure she had his name right, "I realize I am not your average skilled, placeable person, but that's your job, isn't it? Placing people? Or do you expect people just to fall neatly into your job openings?" She rose stiffly, her body appearing tall and straight despite her shapeless suit. "I am sorry I don't fit nicely into a round hole for you. I'm afraid I'm a square peg, but somewhere there is a square opening." She turned toward the door with a firm step.

"Indians," he read aloud. He seemed not to have heard her at all.

"What?" She stopped and turned to face him.

Again he looked up at her over the rim of his glasses. "You wrote that you're interested in Indians."

She felt another put-down coming. "Yes. I find that they are a fascinating people to study and learn from." She emphasized the word "learn."

"Yes, well, that may be," he said, shrugging his shoulders. It was plain he didn't think so. "I just might have a square opening for you." So he *had* heard her. She returned to the chair and waited as he seemed to be trying to recall something. "You said you had some courses in English," he continued. "Any writing?"

"Yes," she admitted. A thread of excitement began to snake through her, which she tried not to show.

"How do you feel about living with your employer?"

"What?" The question was not one Brittany had been at all prepared to hear.

Mr. Simmons enjoyed his little joke as he leafed through the box of cards and pulled out the one he was looking for. "I have a Mr. Kincade here who discovered a box of papers and unbound journals belonging to his great-grandmother. They have something to do with Indians. All sounds like a grade B Western to me. For some reason he wants them organized and typed, but he wants to oversee the entire project himself, and he insists that whomever he hires live at the house."

"Well, I . . ." Brittany hesitated. It would certainly solve her problem of finding living accommodations, but the arrangement was highly unorthodox at best.

Her expression must have said as much, for Mr. Simmons continued with a note of sarcasm, "Mr. Kincade is a very wealthy man and there is a houseful of servants to protect your honor." He did not try to hide his amusement. "Besides, Mr. Kincade is wheelchair-bound. Of course his son is a bit of a womanizer, I hear, but I don't

think you have anything to worry about in that category,"
he added, looking her up and down.

The suit she wore was a size too large and did nothing
to show off the supple figure beneath it. Brittany's thick
ash-blond hair was pinned in a bun at the nape of her
neck, making her seem older than she was. The lack of
makeup did not enhance her beauty. Her mother had
once called her a hidden rose, but Brittany rarely considered how she looked. Living with Jonathan she'd been
too busy to take much time with her appearance, and,
besides, her husband hadn't believed in trying to alter
what nature had given her.

Nevertheless Brittany's thorns showed through. "I can
take care of myself, Mr. Simmons," she told him firmly.
"I'll take the job."

Driving toward the address on the card, high atop
exclusive Tatum Canyon, Brittany began to have second
thoughts. She had learned to deal with a life three steps
ahead of poverty, having been first a minister's daughter
and then a minister's wife. But opulence was totally new
to her, and she wasn't sure how she would deal with it.

As she passed through an iron gate to gain access to
Mr. Kincade's property, she was rewarded with the sight
of the largest house she had ever seen, rising toward the
pearl blue sky at the end of a very long driveway. On
either side stretched lush green lawns in a land where
water was precious. The outside of the mansion, for there
was no other word to describe it, she decided, looked
like a sprawling hacienda.

And the view must be magnificent, Brittany thought
as she drove closer, for the house was perched on top
of a hill, looking majestically down upon its surroundings. For a moment she wondered if she were back in
her little cramped room at the parsonage, dreaming.

As Brittany pulled up to one side of a large courtyard,
a man dressed in a gray uniform appeared at the side of

the house to open the car door for her. She wondered if he spent his day lying in wait for people to approach the house. Taking a deep breath, she walked past a blue and white marble fountain, which dominated the central courtyard, and knocked on the intricately carved front door.

A butler of formal demeanor, also dressed in gray livery, opened the door. When she told him she was from the agency and had come about Mr. Kincade's great-grandmother's journals, he asked her to wait there and went off in search of a "Mr. Etienne."

The house felt cool in comparison to the May heat outside, and as she waited, Brittany took careful note of all the rooms she could see. The high, arched ceiling in the foyer gave a feeling of spaciousness, while the furnishings throughout the house were heavy and massive. Louvered wooden shutters, closed now against the hot sun, covered the windows, and crossed swords hung over a huge stone fireplace.

Brittany did not have long to wait. The echo of firm footsteps on the wood floor warned her of someone's approach. A man in his mid-forties, casually but elegantly dressed in tan slacks and a soft, expensive-looking shirt, appeared at her left. He looked her over for a moment, the quirk in his pencil-thin mustache and the glint in his eyes expressing his surprise. Although confused by his reaction, Brittany tried not to show it. She stood poised and attentive, waiting for further instructions.

"This way, please," the man said with a hint of a Boston accent. She followed the tall, lanky figure into a room lined floor-to-ceiling with books, where he motioned her to sit down before an ornate oak desk. The top of the desk was littered with papers, and a dusty, half-molded box stood next to it on the floor. To Brittany's left, double French doors led outside to a swimming pool that sparkled in the bright sunshine.

"My name is Etienne Barque," the man said crisply as he leaned back in his chair. "I," he paused as if to search for the right word, "run things here for Mr. Kincade. That includes hiring and firing, although, naturally, he does have the last word." He pressed the tips of his fingers together and studied Brittany. "What are your qualifications, Miss . . . ?"

"Brittany Sinclair," she said, half rising in her seat and extending her hand with what she hoped was a warm smile. He barely touched her fingers, which made her decide that, so far, Phoenix was a very cold place. "I'm not sure just what you're looking for in the way of qualifications," she began. "I have a deep interest in the history of the American Indian, particularly the tribes of this region, and I pride myself on being able to organize material very well." Her eyes swept over the piles of papers, and she wondered briefly if, in her zeal to get the job, she was overrating her abilities.

"Have you written anything of significance?" Etienne Barque asked.

Brittany's throat went slightly dry for the first time as she realized how desperately she wanted this opportunity to delve into someone's past history. Her mind raced for an answer that was truthful yet would still satisfy this very proper man.

"No," she said, "I haven't written anything of significance—yet. This will be the first piece," she told him, gaining confidence as she spoke. "I think I could do justice to this project, and that I would find it fascinating."

"Yes, I dare say. So your father was a minister. That gives you something in common with the old gentleman's great-grandmother. So was hers." The deep-set eyes regarded her thoughtfully as his tapered fingers stroked his light brown mustache. "Well, no one else has worked out," he said at last. "You might as well try your hand at it. You understand that you are to live here?" She nodded. He frowned slightly. "Of course, there is a problem. You are a woman."

"Yes, I am," she said, her eyes narrowing a bit. What an odd thing to say. "Why is that a problem?"

"You'll find that Mr. Kincade is rather firm in his belief that only men can accomplish certain tasks. Does that change your mind?" he asked.

Brittany's green eyes flashed with determination to meet the challenge thrown her. "Not in the slightest," she replied staunchly.

"Mr. Kincade is a bit demanding," Etienne warned her.

"I've dealt with demanding men before. My father was one. So was my husband. I can handle Mr. Kincade."

Etienne Barque hid a smile. "One does not 'handle' Mr. Kincade. One obeys."

Brittany took a deep breath. Mistake number one, she thought. "Yes, sir," she said. "I only meant that neither Mr. Kincade's preconceptions nor his demands will deter me from doing a good job."

Etienne nodded knowingly and a smile formed slowly on his lips, making his dark eyes crinkle at the corners and softening his harsh features. Studying him, Brittany decided she would like to get to know him after all. She hoped his change of mood was a good sign.

"Mr. Kincade does have to approve my hiring you," Etienne reminded her.

Brittany smiled and looked him straight in the eyes, trying her best to convey an air of confidence. It wouldn't do to let the man think she was easily intimidated. "I'm looking forward to meeting him," she said.

"Let's get you settled in then—temporarily," he concluded, rising to his feet and once more leading the way through the large house.

Brittany's heels clicked on the parquet floors as they approached a wide, curving staircase. On the steps lay a thick mink-colored carpet, and the walls were covered in a rich, textured wallpaper. Brittany gazed around her with awe and ran her fingers lightly along the polished bannister.

"It is a bit overwhelming the first time, isn't it?" Etienne commented almost kindly.

Brittany nodded. "I'm not even used to a staircase. Where I come from almost everything is on one level."

"And where do you come from?"

"Fifteen mile outside of Chandler," she told him as they arrived at a landing.

Etienne nodded absently as he opened the door to one of the bedrooms. It was obvious to Brittany that, however masculine the rest of the house was, this room had been decorated for a woman. A double canopy bed stood on the far side with a beautiful white-with-blue bedspread. A side chair covered in the same material stood on the left. To the right was a sunken sitting area with two sofas and a writing desk. Blue drapes hung at the windows and area rugs in a lighter blue covered the floors.

"This belonged to Mrs. Kincade when she was alive," Etienne informed her. "Mr. Ambroise's wife." He seemed to need to clarify. "Did you bring your luggage?"

"It's in the car. One suitcase and a large package of books," Brittany answered absently, entranced by her surroundings. Through a door to the far left she glimpsed a huge bathroom with a sunken, tiled bathtub. Was this really to be her room? Would she have it all to herself? But she hadn't actually been hired yet, she reminded herself, and made a conscious effort to dampen her excitement.

"I'll send for your belongings," Etienne told her, leaving her alone to explore the room more thoroughly.

She walked over to the window and sat down on the sofa beneath it. Gently she touched the filmy blue curtains and ran her hands along the smooth upholstery. All this dazzled her. How nice to have such beautiful things around her.

"Keep a cool head, Brittany," she said aloud, hoping that speaking the words would give them added weight. "Trappings aren't everything." She smiled to herself. But they sure do help a lot, she added silently.

"Young woman, this won't do!"

Brittany jumped to her feet at the sound of the gruff, angry voice. In the open doorway an old man with a white beard sat in a motorized wheelchair. His bushy brows were furrowed together as he studied her critically. "It won't do at all!"

"What won't do?" Brittany asked, finally finding her tongue. She felt like Daniel in the lion's den and hastily prepared herself to meet the lion head on.

"You're a woman," the old man accused her, negotiating the chair into the room without an invitation.

"My being a woman keeps being brought up," Brittany shot back, surprising herself. "Are you prejudiced?" The words seemed to jump to her lips of their own accord.

"Yes!" he shouted, his gnarled hands tightening on the chair's controls. "Women have nothing but cotton in their heads. Only met one in my lifetime who had an intelligent thing to say."

What did she have to lose, Brittany decided. "Prepare yourself to meet another one," she told him, facing him squarely.

The old man seemed momentarily taken aback. He knit his brows, studying her carefully. "Think highly of yourself, don't you?" he said testily.

"I know what I'm worth," she answered boldly, wondering where the words were coming from. "Besides, you seem to be curious as to what your great-grandmother had to say, and unless I miss my guess, she was a woman too."

Was that a smile beneath the whiskers? she wondered, beginning to suspect that Mr. Kincade—for that must be who he was—had more bark than bite. The thought made her relax slightly.

He cleared his throat. "What are your qualifications? Etienne tells me you like Indians."

"I more than 'like' Indians, sir," she answered, feeling more confident on familiar ground. "I find the fact that they have survived against tremendous odds fascinating. There's something there to be learned by all of us. I do have some knowledge of several Indian tribes," she added quickly, seeing he wanted more facts.

"Gleaned, no doubt, from grade B Westerns," he said condescendingly, purposely goading her. His blue eyes gleamed with mischief.

Brittany held up her chin proudly. "No, from my studies at college, from reading about them on my own, and from meeting them."

"On reservations?" he asked.

"No, libraries, church meetings, buses. You'd be surprised where they can turn up," she said with amusement.

"Don't patronize me, young lady. I don't like it and I don't like pushy women who strike up conversations with strangers on buses." He scowled darkly and turned his wheelchair around, heading for the door, apparently ending the interview.

"Being friendly isn't pushy, Mr. Kincade," she called after him, determined not to let him have the last word. She stepped quickly in front of his wheelchair, blocking his way. She just couldn't let this chance get away. "Mr. Kincade, I can do a good job for you," she told him, looking him straight in the eye. "I'm sure you've been told I have no degree after my name, but I am genuinely interested in what your great-grandmother had to say about her life with the Indians. Reaching out and touching a mind from the past is the most rewarding experience we can have. It's our common link to the future," she ended imploringly.

Slowly his expression changed, as if he were considering her in a new light. Brittany forced herself to continue to meet his gaze head on, sensing that he would respect a person who wasn't afraid of him.

"Yes, it is," he said a little more softly. "All right, we'll give you a try. You saw the load on the desk downstairs."

"I'm not afraid of work," she told him proudly, unable to keep a happy smile off her face. She'd gotten the job!

"No one intends to frighten you with it," he retorted irritably. He paused as if hunting his memory. "What's your name, girl?"

"Brittany Sinclair," she said warmly.

"All right, Britt," he said, his snapping blue eyes daring her to challenge the masculine nickname. Using it made him more comfortable, she could tell, so she stifled her protest. "Dinner is at seven," he growled at her. "I don't like people who are late."

She was surprised. "I eat with you?" she asked without thinking.

"This isn't a prison, Britt. We don't shove a tray under your door. Of course you eat with me. Dress," he added in a commanding voice as he shifted the controls and the wheelchair began to roll forward.

Brittany stepped to the side. "I never come naked to dinner," she said softly, still smiling.

"You'll do, Britt, you'll do," the old man murmured as a smile twisted his own lips.

As the wheelchair whirred down the hall, Brittany was left to ponder her sudden good fortune. She not only had a job and a beautiful place to stay, she also relished the thought of being able to go through the writings of someone of another generation, perhaps for the very first time since the words had been written. What common feelings would she find there? What revelations about the past? She could hardly wait!

Her thoughts turned to Jonathan for almost the first time since the funeral, and a tinge of guilt came to her for feeling so happy so soon after his death. But then, she reminded herself, theirs had never been a great love. Jonathan had viewed her as more a helpful asset than a woman he longed to have near him. Life was for the living, after all, and for the first time she had the chance to live it for herself.

Unable to suppress her excitement for another moment, she twirled around on her heels with a soft cry of pleasure, her arms spread wide, and collapsed on the sofa, grinning with delight.

chapter

2

DINNER WAS AN EXPERIENCE.

As she stood facing the closet, studying her meager wardrobe, Brittany did not feel quite as confident as she had earlier. Her clothes were appropriate for Rev. Sinclair's wife, but here they seemed out of place, shapeless, and dull. Clothes never made the man, her mother used to say when there was no money for anything new. They never made the woman, either, Brittany reminded herself as she donned her one-piece dark brown dress, wearing it like a badge of courage. She straightened the gold locket she always wore, her one piece of fine jewelry, which had been given to her by her grandmother. Pulling back her shoulders, she marched down the curving staircase toward where she thought the dining room was located.

Brittany wandered around in the vast mansion for several minutes before she found the dining room. She was the last to arrive at the table. Mr. Kincade raised baleful eyes toward her and glanced significantly at the grandfather clock. Although it had not yet chimed seven, the old man's obvious disapproval made her nervous as she stood wondering where she was supposed to sit.

"You have a very large house," she said by way of explanation, hoping to hide the fact that she'd gotten lost.

Mr. Kincade gave a gruff snort and indicated the seat on his left. Brittany sat down, immediately smoothing her linen napkin across her lap—and then looked up into the most handsome face she had ever seen, directly across the table from her.

For a moment the room faded away. Everything faded away except the broad-shouldered man before her. His almost classic face was deeply tanned, and his strong chin had the slightest hint of a cleft. The lashes that framed soulful eyes were thick and black. His lips, full and sensuous, easily pulled into a smile that appeared to have a touch of cynicism. But the dimple in his cheek gave him an almost boyish look. His thick, slightly wavy hair, which just brushed against his white shirt collar, was blacker than a moonless sky.

He must be Mr. Kincade's son, Brittany thought vaguely and had to concentrate not to gape openmouthed at him. His face was turned away from her as he spoke to a woman at his right, who responded in a high, breathy voice and called him Blake.

"I was saying that, since you now know where the dining room is, you won't be late again," Ambroise Kincade repeated when Brittany did not respond.

She jumped a little as his words penetrated and reluctantly she pulled her eyes away from Blake. "I wasn't late," she corrected Ambroise. "It's just seven now."

As if on cue the clock chimed seven times to back her up. Brittany saw Etienne, seated on her left, hide a quick smile.

At the sound of her voice, melodious but firm, Blake had turned from his companion. Now his gaze met Brittany's across the china and crystal. Brittany thought she could gaze into the blue depths of his eyes forever, and was surprised by her reaction. What had come over her?

Blake tore his eyes from Brittany and raised a questioning brow at his father, who was quick to explain.

"If you'd come home more often, you'd know," Ambroise said. "I've just hired Britt to put together your great-great-grandmother's papers."

"Are you still on that kick?" Blake asked, sounding mildly interested. "I thought you gave up when the last man left." He leaned toward Brittany and added in a confidential tone, "He made a larger mess of it than it already was."

Brittany's heart beat faster as he addressed her. Maybe it was the heat, she thought, trying to find an explanation for her unusual feelings.

"Britt thinks she can do better," Ambroise said drily. "One hopes she is better at organizing than she is at finding her way around." He cocked a sardonic eyebrow at her, and she flushed at the way he'd seen through her small deception.

"You got lost?" the woman at Blake's side asked, laughing. "How very funny." She sounded false and insincere to Brittany, as if she'd taken lessons on how to laugh in a certain high-society manner.

"You have a very strange sense of humor, Sheila," Ambroise commented as soup was served. "Perhaps that's why you get along with my son. His idea of a good time is racing about in tiny cars that look like fiber glass sneakers and offer very little protection for his fool neck," he said crossly.

Brittany's vivid green eyes studied the other woman closely. While Brittany had high cheekbones and a delicate bone structure, Sheila looked more vivacious and athletic. She also appeared to be taller. Her tan was deeper and her hair was platinum blond, parted on the side and worn long and loose. It kept falling over Sheila's right eye and she flipped it back in a habitual gesture. Her eyes, unlike Blake's, were a cold, ice-water blue, especially when she turned them toward Brittany.

"I'll be early for dinner next time," Brittany promised, eager to make a good impression.

Ambroise nodded absently, intent on eating, which

recalled Brittany to her own food. She looked down with
dismay at the array of silverware on either side of her
soup bowl, at a momentary loss. Her eye caught Blake's
amused expression. With exaggerated movements he
picked up his soup spoon for her inspection and began
eating. Brittany was embarrassed despite her determination not to be, but she dutifully copied him by picking
up her own soup spoon and dipping it carefully into the
creamy liquid.

"You'll excuse me for asking, Mr. Kincade," Sheila
was saying as Brittany tasted the soup, "but why do you
need anyone to work on those papers? You can read them
yourself. What's she going to do for you?" She spoke
of Brittany as if she were a nonentity, and Brittany found
herself disliking the beautiful woman intensely—more,
her calmer mind judged, than the situation warranted.

"Not that's it's any business of yours, Sheila, but I
don't see all that well anymore." Mr. Kincade's tone was
icy. Although Brittany couldn't understand why, she
would have sworn Ambroise Kincade was coming to her
own defense. He didn't seem to like Sheila any better
than she did. "And I can well afford to pay for the luxury
of having someone plow through those papers and give
some kind of continuity to them. Then I can read them
if I want to, or have them read to me." He turned to
Brittany. "You'll start tomorrow morning." The words
sounded like a royal command.

"I'll be happy to," she replied, thrilled at the approval
implied in his order.

The more Brittany thought about it, the more she
wanted to immerse herself in her work. She had been far
luckier than she had a right to hope for. When she had
gone to the agency that morning, she'd been ready to
settle for almost any nine-to-five job. Instead she'd found
an adventure that promised to expose her to new worlds,
both past and present, that had always been beyond her
grasp.

Her green eyes slid back toward Sheila, who looked cool and sophisticated in a bright pink sun dress held up by two tiny bows on her tanned shoulders. Her platinum hair bounced about her shoulders as she talked to Blake and touched his arm frequently in a possessive way. They were deep into a conversation of their own, leaving Brittany an uninvolved observer. Ambroise began to talk to Etienne about estate matters that needed seeing to. Brittany was left to her thoughts as she ate her dinner. Indeed, no one even noticed whether she used the correct fork.

That night Brittany was too excited to sleep. The clock ticked away next to her bed—eleven, twelve, one.

Finally, after twisting and turning until the sheets were tied in knots, she got up from the bed and slipped on a shapeless blue robe she had brought with her. At least ten years old, it was faded and patched, something that had never bothered Brittany before. But now she looked at it with new eyes and realized just how ratty it must appear to others. Perhaps she could buy a new one once she'd saved some money, but until then it would have to do. After all, just because she was living in a beautiful house didn't mean she should start wanting lots of new clothes.

As Brittany curled up on a sofa and gazed outside at the still desert landscape, her ash-blond hair fell about her shoulders like a cape, catching the shimmer of moonlight that came through her open window.

A restlessness had taken hold of her. She had long since unpacked all her belongings and put them away— everything, that is, except Jonathan's picture. She had taken it with her when she left the parsonage, but there seemed no place for it here. After studying it for a moment, she had placed it back in the cloth suitcase and closed the lid. She felt as if the picture were that of a stranger, and in many ways Jonathan had been a stranger to her. Her father had liked him, possibily because Jon-

athan was like a younger version of himself, and had
urged Brittany to accept the man's proposal...a proposal Brittany was sure now her father had convinced
Jonathan to make. Everything had been tied up neatly,
which was just her father's way. Looking back Brittany
wasn't even sure why she had married Jonathan. Probably because she had hoped that the kindly man would
love her the way she longed to be loved. Instead he had
been considerate but rarely affectionate and certainly
never passionate. Eventually her dreams had died.

Brittany sighed and put her thoughts out of her mind,
seeing no point in dwelling on the past. She was free
now, free for the first time to sample life and to account
to no one—no one but herself.

"'To thine own self be true,'" she whispered softly,
quoting a line from *Hamlet*. Her lips curled up into a
soft, wistful smile.

Her thoughts turned to the work waiting for her downstairs, and her enthusiasm soared. What a wonderful
opportunity, she thought, and suddenly she couldn't wait
to begin reading the time-worn pages.

The house was still and had been for some time, so
she assumed she wouldn't be disturbing anyone if she
went downstairs to the library and took a cursory look
at her work. A preview, she thought, smiling. Mr. Kincade had retired hours ago, and Blake and Sheila had left
for some party or other, so Brittany knew she wasn't
about to run into anyone.

She wondered briefly what sort of a party it was but
forced herself to think of something else. The upstairs
hallway was dimly lit for the night, but she found her
way down the curved stairs to the library without any
trouble. Too bad Sheila couldn't see her now, she
thought, recalling how the other woman had laughed at
her directionlessness. She resented Sheila because she'd
probably never had to work in her life, and she acted so

superior. Funny, but Brittany didn't resent Blake, whose race-car driving could hardly be called a useful job.

Brittany sat down in the big desk chair, switched on an antique lamp, and picked up a group of papers at random. The pages felt stiff and brittle in her fingers. They were more than a hundred years old. The very idea thrilled her. She was touching a piece of paper on which a hundred years ago an unknown woman had poured out her thoughts. Elizabeth McCandles was alive again.

Brittany's eyes strained at the faded letters on the page and she began to read slowly.

June 1, 1877
I am so afraid of the task before me. Father expects so much of me. I expect so much of me and the people here are so strange. It is another world.

Brittany smiled. "Elizabeth, we're going to get along fine, you and I," she whispered into the silent room.

The unexpected grate of a key in the front door made Brittany freeze. She heard the door close and then the faint sound of voices. Immediately she thought of Blake. He was home, and he had brought Sheila back with him. One look at her ragged bathrobe was enough. She couldn't let them see her like this!

Quickly she turned off the desk lamp and made her way up the back stairs, the ones next to the lift installed for Ambroise. It was farther to her room this way, but at least she would avoid confronting Blake and Sheila.

But as she approached her room, Blake came barreling around the corner and all but ran into her. She gasped as he grabbed her upper arms to steady her. He was alone. Apparently the other voice she had heard hadn't been Sheila's after all. For some reason this pleased Brittany greatly.

"Hey, easy now. I wouldn't want to run over my

father's new employee." Blake chuckled, gazing down
at her warmly. She liked his laugh. It was deep and rich.
The heat of his hands penetrated her robe, and his eyes
seemed to linger on the gentle swell of her breasts. Or
was he just noticing how faded the material was, she
wondered.

"I—I was just on my way to bed," Brittany stammered.

"That's a very good place to be going. Mind if I join
you?" he asked, his eyes twinkling mischievously as they
regarded her almost intimately.

He had an easy smile, but she wasn't used to that kind
of talk, and she didn't like what it inferred. Her bearing
stiffened. "I think I'd better go to my room, Mr. Kincade—alone."

Blake chuckled again. "Suit yourself," he said, and
his hand moved up to her loose hair appreciatively. She
pulled back, and a lock of her hair ran across his hand.
"You know, you're really not bad looking, even though
you are a little fuzzy right now."

"I have sound teeth, too," she said, her eyes flashing.
"I'm not used to being appraised like horseflesh, Mr.
Kincade. Now if you'll excuse me—" She pulled away
from his touch and hurried down the hall.

"Blake," he called after her. "It's Blake—if you ever
need anything." His voice was filled with laughter.

Brittany closed the bedroom door behind her and
turned the key. She could still hear Blake laughing to
himself as he went to his own room, and her face turned
crimson from anger. How dare he be that casual with
her! She leaned against the door, relieved to have escaped
him. Oh, what was the matter with her. He was used to
a different kind of woman than her. Besides, she was
here to work, not play.

Suddenly she felt very tired. She was asleep almost
the moment she settled down between the sheets.

* * *

The hot Arizona sun was barely taking hold of the land when Brittany awoke the next morning. Mr. Kincade had said nothing about when breakfast would be served, so she dressed quickly, pulled back her hair, and went downstairs to tackle her assignment. She passed Etienne on the way to the library.

"Breakfast isn't for another hour," he told her, apparently surprised to find her up so early.

"That's all right. I couldn't wait to get started," she told him, opening the door to the library.

"Admirable. I'll have someone bring in some coffee."

She smiled her appreciation and went into the room, which was rather dark. She pulled back the drapes from the French doors. Elizabeth, she thought fondly, noting the stacks of papers that were everywhere, we're going to shed a little light on your life. With that, she sat down at the desk and began sorting papers. There were hundreds of them. Ambroise Kincade's great-grandmother had certainly liked to write. Organization was definitely the key here, Brittany decided, so organize she would. For a few hours she played a kind of solitaire, using the entire room as her gaming table.

"What's all this?" Ambroise demanded to know when he wheeled into the room late that afternoon. He regarded the mess with disapproval. "I thought you said you were good at organizing."

"I am. This is called divide and conquer," Brittany answered with a grin. "There are a lot of years here," she told him, pushing a loose strand of hair out of her eyes. "I'm already making some headway. I've got almost all the papers separated into the proper years. Then," she said with a sigh, "come the months and the days. Lucky for us Elizabeth dated her writing."

"I like your use of the term 'us,'" Ambroise said as

he moved his wheelchair about the room, trying not to roll over anything. Brittany swept some papers carefully out of his way. "You probably think I'm a vain old man, digging into the past this way," he added truculently.

Brittany sensed his need for acceptance and stopped sorting, leaning back against the desk to look at him. "No," she said honestly, "I don't think you're vain. Roots are important."

Her words seemed to spur him on. "I need to know that I'm part of something that came before me," he continued. "That it doesn't just end with dying. I suppose it sounds like a lot of foolishness to you, being as young as you are, but the older you get, the more you want to *know*."

"I understand," she assured him, touched by his confession despite his belligerent tone.

"Humph," he snorted.

She grinned. "No, really, I understand more than that. The past can teach us a lot, and it's nice to know just who you are and where you fit into the scheme of things, who your people were, so to speak. It's especially nice to know if your ancestors were brave like Elizabeth." She glanced at a particularly high pile of papers. "I haven't had time to read very much, but what I have looked at is impressive. Elizabeth was a brave woman. She was captured by the Apaches when they raided the Navajo mission."

"And?" Ambroise asked eagerly. His sharp blue eyes twinkled with interest.

"I haven't gotten very far," Brittany explained, sorry to disappoint him. "But I'll keep you informed about everything I read."

He nodded. "Well, get on with it," he said, waving his hand and turning the wheelchair around. "Oh, by the way, I'm having a birthday on Saturday."

"Congratulations," Brittany replied warmly.

"The party will start at seven thirty."

"I'll be quiet," she promised, picking up a stack of papers and continuing to sort them.

"You'll be there," Ambroise informed her, turning to pierce her with a sharp eye.

"What?" Panic hit her like a cold wave. "I . . . I haven't got anything to wear," she said lamely, voicing the first excuse that came to mind.

"Etienne is taking care of that now." Without further words, Ambroise rolled the wheelchair out of the room.

Brittany's stomach sank into the bottom of her shoes. She couldn't possibly go. She wouldn't fit in with the Kincade's jet-set crowd. Judging from the people she had seen pass by the open library door in just the past few hours, they would all look and dress totally different from her. She'd have nothing to say.

She glanced down at the paper in her hand. What was the matter with her? If Elizabeth could face the Apaches, she guessed she could face some sophisticated society people for a few hours.

The next day Brittany allowed herself a break shortly before noon and explored a little more of the house. Mr. Kincade had gone to a business meeting of some sort with Etienne. Absently she wondered where Blake was. Probably with Sheila. For some reason the idea saddened her.

She wandered from room to room, amazed by what she saw—the vast rooms, the beautiful furniture, the exquisite pieces of art. Finally she came across what appeared to be a family room. Several well-worn sofas, side chairs, and piles of magazines and books suggested to her that someone used this room fairly frequently. It had a comfortable, lived-in look that almost, but not quite, reminded her of the parsonage. But best of all a piano stood off to one side. Brittany ran her fingers lovingly over the keys. How long had it been since she had played? For years she had played for her husband in the evenings and the congregation on Sunday mornings. But only when Jonathan was away on a business trip—usually a weekend retreat or a religious conference—did she let the notes of popular tunes escape and carry her into a world where cares did not exist.

Brittany looked about her. No one was around. She had seen only the butler all day. Feeling a little guilty—for what she wasn't sure—she sat down and began to play, closing her eyes and dreaming...Dreaming of what? As the melody of a popular love song engulfed her, the sight of brilliant blue eyes seized her thoughts. Shimmering blue eyes with just a hint of sadness to them, despite the sparkle, hypnotized her thoughts. Abruptly she stopped and opened her eyes.

"Oh, don't stop now. I kind of like it."

Brittany swung around in her seat to see Blake standing three feet away from her. "Oh, you startled me," she said, feeling like a fool.

"Sorry." He moved nearer and stood over her, leaning a little forward. She could smell the musky scent of his cologne, and it stirred her senses, making her heart beat faster. His teeth looked even whiter against his tanned complexion. "Go on, please," Blake encouraged her.

Brittany withdrew her hands from the keyboard. "No, really, I'm kind of awkward. I play church songs best."

"Which I don't find particularly uplifting," he commented dryly.

"Oh, you'd be surprised," she contradicted. "Some hymns are beautiful—and inspiring no matter what your mood." She was surprised at how defensive she sounded. Why did he always have this effect on her?

"Yes, I probably would be surprised. But that song you were just playing never came up in any hymn book," he told her, sitting down on the piano bench next to her.

Brittany's throat went dry. "Sometimes when my husband wasn't around I'd play popular songs," she admitted, just for something to say. Blake's nearness made her uncomfortable. She rose and turned to leave.

"Your husband?" Blake repeated, catching her wrist to stop her. "Are you divorced?" To Brittany's surprise he sounded almost hopeful.

"I'm widowed. My husband died about two months ago."

Blake looked at her, a serious light coming into his shimmering blue eyes. "I'm sorry," he said quietly, sincerely, as if he meant it. Brittany's heart twisted at his unexpected concern. "Well, go on playing, please. I didn't mean to scare you away," he added with a laugh, his somber mood leaving as quickly as it had come. With seeming reluctance he let go of her wrist.

Brittany turned abruptly on her heel, suddenly angry at the slight put-down. "I don't scare easily, Blake," she told him firmly. "I just have work to do." And with that, she left.

She had called him Blake. How easily the name had come to her lips. How nice it felt. She brought herself up sharply. Blake Kincade was a charming playboy and far beyond her reach. The sooner she realized that the better. Work, Brittany, work, she commanded herself.

She worked far past lunch.

Saturday, the day of Ambroise's party, came all too soon. Brittany stood in her room, staring reluctantly down at the dress Etienne had laid out on the bed for her. It was beautiful, but how could she accept such an expensive gift?

"How did you know my size?" she wanted to know. Etienne had never even asked her.

A flicker of a satisfied smile flashed beneath the pencil-thin mustache. "My father was a tailor, and before I ran off to make my mark in the world I learned a lot from him, although at the time I would never have admitted it. I even had a fling at working for a dress designer. The models were frozen women—I ought to know, I married three of them—and the pressure was too much. Did I answer all your questions?" he concluded formally.

"Actually, you raised a lot more," she said, but she swept them all to the back of her mind as she gazed at the mint-green dress, a fringed paisley shawl lying next to it. Neatly arranged beneath the bed were matching shoes. The dress was the most beautiful garment Brittany had ever seen, but again a twinge of guilt pushed past her excitement. She looked up at Etienne.

"It highlights your eyes," he commented noncommitally.

"The dress is lovely, Etienne, and I appreciate the time you took to choose it for me, but I can't accept it. I can't possibly pay for it," she protested.

"No one is asking you to," he told her warmly, seeming to sympathize with her dilemma. "Mr. Kincade enjoys being frivolous once in a while. You're the first woman he's spent money on in a long, long time. Enjoy it."

"I've never had anything like this," she admitted, running her hand gently over the soft material. It felt as delightful as it looked.

"I'm sure all your clothes are sensible," Etienne said. "That was why the old gentleman sent me out instead of you. Here." He opened a box he had under his arm. "I'm sure you'll find everything you need here." Brittany looked down on a collection of makeup. "When in Rome..." Etienne told her, putting the box into her hands. "Now get ready. You've only a couple of hours left before the guests start arriving."

Brittany continued to look thoughtfully down at her possessions, wondering desperately how she could get out of this. She wasn't even sure she knew how to put on all the makeup.

"I can see what you're thinking." Etienne interrupted her thoughts. "Yes, you will be missed and, no, you can't stay in your room. I shall come up and get you if you're not down in time."

With that, he left her contemplating the situation. Tentatively she lifted the dress, then held it up to herself in front of the mirror. "Oh no!" She shook her head. The dress was cut much too low. She couldn't possibly wear it . . . Or could she? Slowly a smile came to her full lips.

She showered quickly and, settling comfortably on a stool in the dressing area of her bedroom, she put on her best bra and panties and the only half-slip she owned. Carefully she drew on new pantyhose. Finally she faced her dress as if it were something to be approached slowly. Perhaps it wouldn't fit and then she'd have an excuse not to attend the party. Coward, her mind taunted her. Was she afraid? Afraid of Sheila? She stopped. Now why had she thought of that? Because she wanted to impress Blake. Like it or not, she was attracted to him.

She looked at herself in the three-way mirror in surprise, feeling an excited tingle, something she had never experienced before during all her time with Jonathan. Making a decision, she reached bravely for the makeup case.

To her delight, Brittany found she had a natural flair for makeup. The result made her step back and look at herself as if for the first time. She was actually pretty. More than that, she was almost beautiful. Growing up in her father's house, she had been taught that such thoughts were vain, not proper for a young woman. No one had ever suggested she was the least bit attractive. Even her mother, a kind, loving woman who had died before Brittany was twelve, had always stressed inner beauty alone. But the image in the mirror pleased Brittany greatly. Her almond-shaped green eyes made her look exotic and mysterious. With mounting enthusiasm, she lifted the dress over her head.

It fit snugly and something within Brittany glowed happily. But the image in the mirror did not look like her at all. Gone were the sensible shoes and loose, somber clothing that fit any occasion. This dress hugged her curves, which were generous and well-proportioned. A wicked slit up the side of the dress exposed a well-formed thigh. Brittany turned around slowly in front of the mirrors, which showed her off from every angle. Why, she looked every bit as feminine as Sheila—perhaps even more so. Sheila was more sophisticated, but she was softer.

But when Brittany's eyes fell again on the plunging neckline, she flushed with dismay. Cut deeply in back, the dress was only a little higher in front. What was Etienne trying to do to her, she wondered, beginning to arrange the paisley shawl to cover as much of her exposed bosom as possible. Now she had to find a way to secure it permanently.

A knock sounded on the door. Etienne must have come to see his handiwork, Brittany thought, a little annoyed. She was going to be so self-conscious all evening. "Come in," she called, fiddling with the white fringes.

The door opened behind her and she looked up sharply at Blake, looking very handsome in a dark suit and a ruffled blue shirt that accented his eyes. His hips were slim in perfectly tailored trousers, and his shoulders were powerful and broad. Brittany's heart skipped a beat.

Blake's expression was one of surprise. "I take it this is your first low-cut gown," he said with amusement, noticing her awkward efforts to arrange the shawl. His eyes drifted down the length of her slender body with new appreciation.

Brittany pulled the ends of the shawl closer together, embarrassed and annoyed at his tone. "I'm used to more material, if that's what you mean," she retorted dryly.

In two strides Blake was directly before her, taking

her hands and spreading them back—and with them, the shawl. Revealed to his view was her deep cleavage and the plane of her firm, high breasts. "You shouldn't hide behind this," he told her, taking the shawl from her hands. "This dress becomes you far more than what you've been wearing." He stepped slightly back for a moment and framed her face with his hands, as if he were taking a picture. "Wait, there's something wrong."

Flustered and annoyed, Brittany began, "I may not look like the..." but he wasn't listening and her voice trailed off.

He'd moved close to her again and her blood began to surge. She must be scarlet by now, she thought angrily. What was the matter with her? She had always been in such control of herself before. Her father had always said no one knew what she was thinking—and at times that had been a good thing, for although on the surface she'd been a model daughter and then wife, in the last few years she'd felt stirrings of dissatisfaction with her life. Something had been missing. Something like the excitement she now felt standing next to Blake, she suddenly realized.

Now Blake's hands were moving to her blond hair. Deftly he took out the three pins that secured it in a tight knot at the back of her neck.

"What are you doing?" she demanded, furious at his high-handedness. He had no right to touch her like this.

"I'm making a vision of you," he said as her hair tumbled down in a soft cloud about her shoulders. He stroked the long length of it, his breath caressing her face, sending pulsating ripples of heat down to her fingertips and robbing her of her angry words. He gazed down at her with a strange look on his face—a look she didn't understand at all—and for a fleeting moment she thought he was going to kiss her.

"Ah, so you are ready," said a voice in the doorway. Startled, they looked up, the intimate moment shattered. Etienne strode into the room, appearing very pleased with himself. "Perfect fit. What did I tell you?"

"It's too small," Brittany protested.

"It's perfect," Blake contradicted and, despite herself, she was thrilled. The sensible side of her reminded her that Blake had probably said that to countless women before her. Her father had always told her there were two kinds of men—the marrying kind and the playboys. The words of the latter were never to be taken to heart, for they were never sincere. Brittany struggled to remember that now.

"Shall we?" Blake asked, extending his arm to her.

She took hold of it lightly, and he pulled her a little closer to his side. "I wouldn't want you to fall on those brand new shoes," he said, grinning wickedly.

He was mocking her, she realized angrily, and pulled her hand free. How dare he make fun of her! "I'm perfectly capable of walking by myself, thank you," she told him, striding ahead of the two men. But her heart gave a slight twinge. Why was Blake always laughing at her? Was she really such a country bumpkin? Or was he simply cruel and insensitive—a handsome but dangerous man?

Brittany glanced over her shoulder to see if Blake was angry, but he merely looked amused as he followed her down the stairs. She faced forward once again and walked down erect and proud.

chapter
3

SHEILA WAS ONE of the first people Brittany saw as she entered the large, festively decorated ballroom. The other woman was wearing a strapless white gown which offset her tan and made her look like a haughty goddess. This impression was heightened by the superior look on her face as she came forward to claim Blake from Brittany.

"Darling, have you been on a mission of charity?" Sheila asked, looking Brittany over critically. "Needs a little more work, I'm afraid." She laughed, then turned away and pulled Blake onto the dance floor. "You promised me the first dance," she cooed.

Blake glanced over Sheila's shoulder at Brittany, but she turned her face away, not wanting to see them in each other's arms.

Ambroise rolled his wheelchair toward Brittany. "Well, well, well," he said. "It seems the butterfly has emerged." He nodded his approval at Etienne. "You've succeeded admirably." His praise brought a smile to Brittany's lips. Since she had more or less agreed to accept his generous gift of the dress, she was glad he was pleased with the results.

"I just picked the trappings, the model is excellent," Etienne commented. Brittany's face glowed.

"Much better," Ambroise commented, apparently

meaning her smile. "I'll have no frowning at my party. If anyone should be frowning, it's me. Seventy-two." He shook his head.

"Age is a number that tries to enslave you," Etienne told him philosophically. Brittany was amused by his formal manner.

"Speaking of slaves, why don't you cut in on Blake?" Ambroise said. It was more of a command than a suggestion. "If I remember correctly, you can be charming when you want to be."

Brittany had a sudden desire to lose herself in the gaily clothed crowd. There had been far fewer people at the church gatherings she'd attended with Jonathan than she saw tonight. But Ambroise had taken hold of her hand.

"You really do look lovely," he said. "Let an old man rest his eyes on something soft and beautiful."

She wasn't used to compliments. "You're just being kind," she told him, embarrassed.

"My dear, I am never kind. I only say what I see. Ah, here's my wayward son. Blake, what do you think of my butterfly?" he asked, holding up her hand.

"This is one of your better projects," Blake said to his father, never taking his eyes off Brittany. "May I have what's left of this dance?"

"I—" She began to protest, but found herself engulfed in his strong arms and suddenly whisked away to the strains of a romantic slow song. She tried to keep a slight distance between them, but failed as he pulled her close to him, the warmth of his body penetrating her clothing, heightening her senses until she was painfully aware of the thud of his heart so close to her own and the hardness of his thighs moving against hers.

"Don't be so afraid of me. I don't bite," he teased, seeming to have sensed her uneasiness.

"I'm not afraid," she contradicted automatically, lifting her chin in a proud gesture.

"Then why are you trying to leave enough space between us to run a train through?" he asked, highly amused. His arms tightened around her, drawing her closer.

She forced herself to relax and molded her body against his. "Better?" she asked, rising to his challenge, her green eyes creating a dare of her own.

"Much," he whispered into her hair, his breath brushing against her temple and sending a shiver down her spine. The silence between them was a comfortable one, and Brittany thought she could dance in his arms forever.

"Blake, be a lamb and get me a drink. I'm so thirsty."

They looked up to find Sheila standing next to them. Brittany stepped back as Blake released his hold on her.

"Would you like one too?" he asked Brittany.

She shook her head, disoriented from the sudden interruption.

"You can't serve drinks to minors, Blake," Sheila said with a smirk. She ran her pale blue eyes contemptuously over Brittany.

"I'm twenty-four," Brittany informed her, annoyed.

Sheila gave her a frosty look. "Oh? The way you keep trying to change your appearance, I really can't guess what age you are. Nor do I care. Do I get my drink, honey?" she asked, turning a softer expression toward Blake. "I'll have what we had last night in my apartment." She cast a sly glance toward Brittany as Blake headed for the bar.

Suddenly Etienne arrived at Brittany's side and took her off to meet some people. "You're not alone. No one likes her," he said, guiding her by the elbow.

"Blake seems to," she said, trying not to sound as if it mattered.

"Blake likes excitement. Fast cars—"

"And fast women," Brittany interrupted with only a touch of bitterness as she watched him return to Sheila with a drink. She tried not to think about him as Etienne introduced her to a lively group of people. Soon she was chatting easily with a jovial man who turned out to be one of Ambroise's business associates.

Shortly thereafter a small army of waiters rolled out a huge cake on a wheeled trolley; and the crowd gathered around it to sing "Happy Birthday." Although Ambroise tried to maintain his usual stern expression, Brittany could tell he was thriving on all the attention.

"Why don't you have Brittany play "Happy Birthday" for you on the piano, dad?" Blake suggested, pinning her with a teasing grin.

"You play?" Ambroise asked, twisting in his chair to look at her standing behind him. Brittany shook her head in protest, not wanting to play for all these sophisticated people, but before she could voice her reluctance Blake spoke for her.

"She plays the piano quite well," he said. She shot him a dirty look.

"Well, then, by all means. You there, stand up," Ambroise ordered the man seated at the piano, who was part of the orchestra he had hired for the evening. The musician did as bidden and stepped aside for Brittany.

She felt all eyes on her as she sat down. She began haltingly. Then, catching the smirk on Sheila's face, she attacked the keys with new determination until the notes rang out, rich and full. The party-goers sang along, filling the room with exuberant good cheer.

Etienne seemed to have caught the eye play between the two women. "It's the first time "Happy Birthday" was ever played with a vengeance," Brittany overheard him comment to Ambroise above the din. The older man chuckled, obviously enjoying himself.

"You," he shouted, pointing to Blake when the song was over, "blow out my candles."

"Dad, it's not the same if I do it," Blake protested, laughing along with the rest of the group.

"You're more full of hot air than I am," Ambroise retorted, and the group broke up again. Brittany began to rise gratefully from the piano bench but Ambroise interrupted. "No, play something else, Britt. I like the piano."

Obediently she sat down again and began playing something light, as Blake blew out all the candles for his father and the crowd burst into applause. Gradually she became aware that Blake was watching her, that he was working his way through the crowd to her side. Again she grew self-conscious under his warm regard.

"Do you mind?" he asked, sitting down next to her on the bench. "I like to play, too."

"I already know that," she quipped, trying to hide her heightened awareness of him.

He laughed. "So you do."

As he began picking out the tune she was playing, she wondered how his large hands could caress the keys so lightly. She felt his thigh press against hers as it moved in rhythm to the music and nearly forgot which notes to play. She slid away from him and found herself on the very edge of the bench.

"You're pushing me off the seat," she said between clenched teeth so that the people gathering in front of them wouldn't hear.

"Then stop moving away," he told her, flashing a wicked smile. She glared down at the keys as she tried to keep pace with him.

"Play louder!" Ambroise called over the noise of the crowd, thumping his hand on the arm of the wheelchair in time to the music. Brittany pounded the keys, but Blake easily matched her, and she began to sense that they were competing in an unspoken contest.

At the end of another song, Brittany began to rise once more. "I think you can carry on without me," she told Blake, conceding the victory to him.

He caught her hand. "I'd rather carry on *with* you," he murmured huskily.

She pressed her lips together, determined to resist him. "Sheila's waiting."

"Sheila can take care of herself," he assured her. "Danny," he called, catching the attention of one of his friends, "do me a favor. Dance with Sheila, will you?"

"My pleasure," the man named Danny said and went off in search of his partner.

"Aren't you ashamed of yourself?" Brittany asked, thoroughly exasperated with his high-handedness.

"Never," Blake replied easily, taking hold of her arm. Her cleavage deepened as she got up, and for a moment his eyes didn't meet her face. "Never," he repeated, catching the look she gave him. He guided her firmly away from the crowd.

"Where are you taking me?" she wanted to know, suddenly suspicious.

"To my tent, fair maiden, stretched out beneath the Arabian sky," he said, twirling an imaginary mustache. "Or to the terrace, since it's closer. I thought you might like a bit of fresh air. The sun's down, so it's cooler. And the view—well, come with me." His hand slid slowly down her arm and became entangled with her fingers as he led her into another room and through a set of French doors. He closed them behind him and Brittany found herself on a terrace suspended above a steep cliff.

"Let them enjoy the air-conditioning," Blake said, indicating the party-goers. "I like it better here."

She followed his gaze upward. Hundreds of stars were shining in the clear sky, winking down at them. The night air was still—except for the beating of her heart, Brittany thought ruefully. The muffled sounds of the party reached them as if from a great distance.

"It really is kind of nice out here, isn't it?" Blake said. "Look down. The entire city is at your feet."

And so it appeared to be. The lights of the city below shone like a dazzling diamond crown, a myriad of lights reflecting back to the stars that looked down on them.

"It's breathtaking," Brittany whispered with awe.

"I'll tell you what's breathtaking—you are," he said quietly, gently pushing a strand of hair away from her face.

"I can't be that breathtaking since you're still breathing," she said, trying to keep her voice light and her pulse calm.

"Only through superhuman effort," he assured her with a smile. Casually he put his arm around her as he pointed out the view. "We're suspended out here between the sky and the land, just you and me."

"And four hundred intimate friends," she retorted.

"They're locked inside," he reminded her.

He ran his finger along the length of her cheek, then crooked it beneath her chin. She felt an uncontrollable flutter of excitement take hold of her as he lifted her mouth and bent his own to meet it. Ever so gently his lips brushed against hers, causing a fire to spring up within her. Another kiss followed the first, less gentle, more urgent. Slowly he drew her into his arms and pressed his mouth against hers as a sweeping fire took hold of her. Something within her rose up to meet him as her senses reeled and her mind totally floated away. Another wave of fire went over her as the kiss became more and more intense and she found her breath all but gone.

She opened her eyes and, to her surprise, found herself just where she had been, not hurtling through space, as she had thought, or drifting on a cloud, which would have been more in keeping with what she felt inside. Blake's eyes shone in the moonlight like twin pieces of sky, beckoning to her. They held amusement—and just a hint of something else. Could it be sadness?

"Blake, I've been looking all over for you."

Brittany all but jumped at the sound of Sheila's voice. The other woman had a cold smile on her lips as she looked at Blake. "You promised me a ride in the moonlight, remember?"

"Later, Sheila," Blake said, obviously annoyed. But the intimate moment between them had already been ruined.

Brittany was amazed by Sheila's uncanny ability to find her and Blake together. This was the third time she had done so.

"The party's getting boring, darling. Can't we go now? Please?" Sheila pouted.

Blake looked down at Brittany, apparently undecided, and she took a step back from him. "Don't let me stand in your way," she said, her voice cold to hide her hurt. She couldn't understand why he was the least bit interested in Sheila, but if he had even a moment's hesitation in choosing between them, she would make the choice for him. She refused to compete with the blond woman— especially for the attentions of a man like Blake Kincade.

"Alright," Blake told Sheila. "I'll bring the car up to the front."

"The silver one, darling. It flies under your touch— just like I do," she purred. Brittany rolled her eyes at Sheila's obvious innuendo. How could Blake allow himself to be taken in by her? Brittany sensed an anger in him barely held in check, but he only breathed in deeply before striding through the glass doors.

Sheila's expression hardened the moment Blake was gone, and she took hold of Brittany's arm. "Now you listen to me. I don't know what your little game is, but Blake is mine, do you hear me?"

"Does he know that?" Brittany asked, pulling her arm free, angry now at both Blake and Sheila.

The other woman flashed a deep emerald ring on her left hand. "Just what do you think this is?" she demanded.

"A very pretty ring," Brittany said dryly, hardly looking at it.

"Yes, and Blake got it for me. It's my engagement ring. Diamonds are so common," Sheila said haughtily.

"You're engaged?" Brittany asked, stunned in spite of her determination not to care. How could Blake have kissed her like that if . . . if he didn't mean it, if he were engaged to someone else? He must have been laughing at her all the time.

"I said so, didn't I?" Sheila continued. "Now, are you going to be a good girl and run along, or do I have to get nasty with you?"

"I think you've been quite nasty enough already," Brittany replied with a haughtiness all her own. She brushed past Sheila without another look.

Engaged. Blake was engaged. The words sounded over and over again in her head. Well, that was what she got for letting go of her feelings. Anger at her own naiveté overwhelmed her. She had let a man kiss her passionately, a man who had already committed himself to another woman, a man who saw her only as another in a long string of conquests. Oh, he was charming alright. Charming and handsome and very skilled in seducing inexperienced women like herself. But he would never touch her again. He'd never have the chance. She'd see to that.

"Is anything wrong, my dear?"

Brittany looked up to find she had almost walked into Etienne, who loomed over her like a tall, somber street lamp. She shook her head and managed a weak smile. "I'm just a little tired, that's all."

"You need a drink," he said wisely, steering her toward the bar.

"I don't really—"

"Sometimes it helps," he interrupted, leaving her side and returning moments later with a screwdriver, before she had time to say no. "Drink up," he told her. "There's vitamin C in it. Keeps you healthy. And after that you'll do me the honor of dancing with me and wiping away that sour look."

Brittany had to smile and do as she was bidden. It felt nice to be pampered. The drink, which was very mild upon Etienne's expressed orders, did taste good. But the slightly heady feeling it gave her didn't hold a candle to the way Blake's kiss had made her feel. Blake. She had to stop thinking about him. It was time she grew up and realized that life was full of disappointments. With renewed determination Brittany put down the glass and offered up her hands to Etienne. "I'm ready to dance," she told him.

Etienne whirled her expertly about the floor until several eligible bachelors cut in on him, each smoother than the last. But try as she might, Brittany couldn't help comparing them to Blake. No one stood a chance.

The party had broken up several hours ago and, though dawn was only a little while off, Brittany was still not tired, only sad. The feel of Blake's kiss was still on her lips. She stood alone in the massive living room's conversation pit, looking into the empty fireplace. That was all her dreams would lead to if she gave in to her feelings—cold emptiness. She sighed. Why did he have to be so irresistibly good-looking? Why . . .

"Hi. You're still up."

She didn't have to turn around to know that the deep voice was Blake's. Her initial, unguarded thrill dissolved into anger. She wasn't about to be played for a fool again.

"I was just going to bed," she said curtly, turning to leave.

Blake was beside her more quickly than she would have thought possible. "Mind if I join you?" he asked with deceptive casualness.

"You're impossible!" she retorted.

"I can be managed by the right hands," he said, picking up one of hers and kissing it ever so lightly.

She pulled it back. "What about Sheila's hands?" she retorted angrily.

"They're not as pretty as yours," he told her, running his fingers up her shoulder and resting them on one of the thin straps holding up the green dress. He kissed her tenderly there, sending a tremor through her whole body. Brittany tried to move away, but suddenly found that he had pinned her against the fireplace. Her body ached to be held against him again even as her mind screamed no. "I felt something in your kiss tonight," Blake told her, his face not more than an inch away from hers.

"What you felt was your own imagination. There was nothing there," she said defensively.

"I think there was." He spoke quietly, sincerely, without lessening his hold on her. A devilish grin creased his handsome face and his eyes twinkled. "What would you do," he asked, toying with one shoulder strap, "if I just tugged at this a little?" Playfully, he began to do so.

"I'd scream so fast that half the house would be down here in a second," she told him, pulling his hand away. Her skin burned where he had touched her.

"No, you wouldn't . . ."

"Want to bet?" she snapped.

"You wouldn't because I'd stop you, like this." And his mouth covered hers, pressing insistently, drawing her out of herself, wooing her, calling to her until again she was lost in his kiss. His body molded to hers as he lifted her arms and placed them about his neck. Suddenly she was clinging to him and running her hands through his thick, raven-black hair.

You're a fool, she told herself over and over again, trying to pull herself back from the abyss toward which she was hurtling. She might have one night of ecstasy or whatever there was at the end of the fiery tunnel he was leading her through, and then he'd go back to Sheila and marry her, having had a good laugh. No! She mustn't let him use her like that!

With what felt like her last ounce of strength, Brittany managed to pull away. "No, no, I won't be a statistic, a notch in your belt, a feather in your cap . . ." Her voice trailed off as she tried to catch her breath.

"Well, now that you've exhausted all the metaphors, what do you take me for?" Blake wasn't angry, only amused, which incensed her all the more. Obviously this was only a game to him.

"You know what you are," she replied coldly, turning on her heel and hurrying away before her heart made her stay.

She passed Etienne on the way out. He gave her a quizzical look, but she couldn't bring herself to say anything. She just wanted to be alone.

"Etienne," she heard Blake say with a chuckle as she raced up the stairs, "you've hired us a hellcat. Thanks."

At that moment she almost hated him.

Brittany threw herself down on the bed, and for the first time since her husband had died, she allowed herself the luxury of tears. She cried for herself, for the frustrated desire that beat in her breast, and for the fact that Blake was far out of her reach. She couldn't have him. She shouldn't want him. And amid all this she thought of her late husband. In all her married life not one kiss from him, not all his kisses put together, had made her feel the way one of Blake's kisses had. Blake had opened up a whole new world to her, and she knew that she would never again be satisfied with the fleeting caresses of a preoccupied man. For if she were honest with herself, that was the way it had been most of the time with Jonathan. She realized now that they had shared a mutual respect, but never love. Not the kind of love she felt now. She dried her eyes and sat up.

Brittany looked at her reflection in the mirror across

the room and saw a face flushed from crying—or was her high color a lingering effect of Blake's kiss?

"Brittany, my girl, your education didn't cover this part," she said out loud. "Welcome to the real world."

"Well, you certainly don't look the worse for wear," Etienne commented, entering the library with a cup of coffee at nine thirty the next morning. "I wasn't sure I'd even find you here after last night. Here." He pushed the coffee toward her. "I think you need this."

"Is it Irish coffee?" she asked, remembering the screwdriver he had given her the night before.

"No, it's too early for that." He smiled. "We don't want to turn you into an alcoholic." Brittany smiled back at him, then turned serious.

"Does Blake race very often?" she asked unexpectedly, surprising herself as much as Etienne with the question. She knew her feelings for Blake must be obvious and felt uncomfortable talking about him.

Etienne appeared not to notice her uneasiness as he considered the question. "Yes, Blake races a great deal. He's been racing now for almost five years, and rather than letting up he's become more involved in it. He's racing tomorrow as a matter of fact."

"He's racing tomorrow?" she echoed in surprise.

Etienne nodded. "He's gone already. Some local thing. He won't miss a single race. His father disapproves greatly."

"I certainly can't blame him," Brittany commented, shuffling papers, pretending to be working. Her thoughts refused to settle down long enough this morning to get involved with Elizabeth for more than a few moments at a time. On one hand she was relieved to learn that Blake was gone from the house. After last night she wasn't sure she could face him with equanimity. On the other hand she feared for his safety. Her husband had died in a terrible car crash less than two months ago, and the thought of Blake facing a similar fate left her feeling physically ill.

"Blake does have a reason for acting the way he does," Etienne went on after a moment, his voice sounding a little less detached than it normally did.

Brittany looked up with interest. "How could anyone have a reason to try to kill themselves by whizzing around at top speed?" she demanded.

Etienne paused. "Blake's wife died of a brain tumor five years ago. They'd only been married for five months. It happened just like that. She fainted while they were out on the beach. She was dead that night, dying in his arms at the hospital. He loved her a great deal."

Brittany stared at Etienne, stunned into speechlessness. Suddenly her own tragedy shrank into insignificance. "I didn't even know he had been married," she said slowly, trying to assimilate the information. She had thought of Blake as a spoiled playboy, charming and irresponsible, untouched by human tragedy. Suddenly she saw him in a whole new light, and the desire she felt for him became colored with sympathy, turning her feelings for him in an even more dangerous direction than before.

Etienne halted in the doorway for a moment. "Blake's wife looked a little like you as a matter of fact." He let the words sink in and then walked out, leaving her bewildered and confused.

Brittany sat very quietly amid the century-old papers, staring straight ahead without seeing anything. Her anger and frustration melted away as she thought of how Blake must have suffered to have loved someone and to have lost her so soon and so tragically. Perhaps Brittany had been too hard on him. Perhaps, in time . . .

Time. Brittany glanced down at the page before her and realized ruefully that she was allowing her personal feelings to get in the way of the job she was being paid to do. With new resolve she tackled the stacks of papers before her.

About twenty piles of paper stood there, representing all the years Elizabeth had either kept a current journal or had written about earlier years from some later point in her life. Now all Brittany had to do was organize the months within each year. All. A smile curled her lips. She'd be lucky to finish the job in the next week.

And then she would get acquainted with Elizabeth McCandles.

Brittany was glad her present work did not require a great deal of concentration because she found herself thinking about Blake's race and worrying. Painful memories of how Jonathan had died returned to her. She imagined him lying battered and broken by the side of the road. And somehow his body became Blake's, twisted almost beyond recognition, and her heart filled with anguish.

Mechanically she arranged the pages written in 1877 into twelve piles and sorted each chronologically by date. The task was boring, but it kept her busy, and every now and then she stopped to read a little, picking up snatches of Elizabeth's life. Already she had learned that Elizabeth had come with her mother and father to serve as a missionary amid the Navajo Indians. Eventually she had been kidnapped in a raid by the dreaded warriors of the plains, the Apaches, who had once been of the same tribe as the Navajos but had long since broken away, scorning the Navajo's peaceful ways.

The raiding party, led by Cochise's son, Nachise, wiped out the little wooden mission, burning it to the ground and killing Elizabeth's parents and the other white couple who had joined them there. Elizabeth's own life was spared at the last moment by Nachise, who ordered that the knife be removed from her throat. Nachise took her prisoner instead.

As it turned out, though initially scorned and abused

by the women of the tribe, Elizabeth soon became a highly prized trophy in the tepee of Nachise. A white squaw was regarded as very valuable, particularly one with blond hair and blue eyes.

Brittany read on, utterly fascinated.

As she worked the next day, Brittany found herself straining to hear the sound of an approaching sports car. She had learned to recognize the roar of Blake's favorite car, the silver Ferrari that hugged the road as if it were one with it. Lunchtime came and went and so did supper, and still Blake did not appear. Brittany began to fear the worst and could see by Ambroise's preoccupation at dinner that, although he talked of business matters with Etienne, his mind was somewhere on a racetrack, worrying about a son who did not worry about himself.

"Damned young whelp," Ambroise muttered over coffee. "Doesn't he know what he's putting me through?"

"Have you tried telling him?" Brittany asked gently.

"I thought you were smart, Britt," he said with a critical edge to his voice. Her eyes held his boldly in a silent challenge, and he softened his tone at once. "You don't tell Blake not to do something. It spurs him on. He's been headstrong ever since he was born. Life always had to be his way. It certainly was a shock when Anne died—Etienne told me you knew. He raged against God, but mostly against himself, as if her death were some kind of punishment meant for him. And then . . ." Ambroise looked into space, not seeing Brittany for a moment. "And then he got the old devil in his eye again, but this time it was different. This time he pulled out all the stops. He's going to be the death of me—as well as himself," he finished sadly. Finally he seemed to become aware of who he was talking to—a stranger. Brittany looked away so that he wouldn't feel embarrassed.

Just then the door opened and Brittany's heart skipped a beat. Blake!

"I won, dad," he shouted triumphantly, holding a silver trophy high over his head. He was still dressed in his racing coveralls, which were smudged and dusty, but to Brittany he looked like a warrior returning victorious from battle. And then Sheila came up behind him and took his arm, and all the joy drained out of Brittany.

She rose gracefully and excused herself politely, leaving the room before Blake could say anything more. But not before she saw the gleam of triumph shining in Sheila's pale blue eyes.

chapter
4

BRITTANY TRIED TO throw herself into the project of reconstructing Elizabeth's life from her papers, but she found that she was now referring to Elizabeth as Blake's relative rather than Ambroise's. Everything seemed to revolve around Blake in one way or another, as sudden flashes of his kisses would abruptly take hold of her mind.

And then there he was the next day, standing in the doorway of the library. She sensed his presence before he said a word, and her shoulders tightened as she tried to ignore him.

"Working pretty diligently, aren't you, Sacajawea?" Blake said.

Brittany glanced up, pretending to have been absorbed in her work. But his dazzling blue eyes began to work their magic, and she turned quickly back to the paper to avoid them. "Sacajawea was a Shoshoni Indian who guided Lewis and Clark to the Oregon territory," she told him. "Elizabeth's journals are about Navajos and Apaches."

Blake leaned over her shoulder to look down at the paper before her. "Fascinating," he murmured teasingly. She smelled his cologne, the same scent he'd worn the night of the party, and it brought a bittersweet pang to her heart. "See, I'm learning things already. Come teach me some more," he entreated, taking her hand.

"Blake, your father is paying me to work," she protested, trying to pull away.

"My father has an awful lot of money to spare, so a few stolen hours won't matter," he told her.

"What are you talking about?"

He snatched the manuscript she'd been reading out from under her nose and held it behind his back. "Now you don't have any work to do, so we can go for a drive. Ah, I see you've kept your hair down for me."

Her hand flew self-consciously to the thick mass of ash-blond locks tumbling about her shoulders. "I just didn't have time to—"

"Uh-huh." He ran his hand over it. "Keep not having time," he told her. His slightly crooked smile thrilled her, seeming to light up the room. She took hold of herself and tried to reach for the manuscript, but he held it high over her head where she couldn't reach it. Exasperated, and too aware of his nearness, she gave up trying to get it and scowled darkly instead.

"You can't have this back until you promise to spend the afternoon with me. You take life much too seriously," Blake reprimanded her.

"Well, you certainly can't be accused of that," she told him, remembering the race and Sheila.

"And what's wrong with a little fun?" he asked beguilingly, trying to take her hand again.

"Nothing, except when it involves a mindless disregard for your own life..."

"You touch me deeply," he said with mock drama, placing his hands over his heart. "Does that mean you care?"

"You'd break your father's heart if something happened to you," she retorted, evading his question, annoyed that he had come upon the real answer so quickly.

"Ah, yes, my father. Don't worry about old Ambroise. He's got a heart of stone, although you certainly managed to knock a chink into it. He likes you, Sacajawea, and

I must admit the old fox has taste. Now, do I get that promise?"

"Where would we go?" Brittany asked despite herself.

"Aha, interest. Good start. We'll go sailing," Blake told her, sitting down on the desk deliberately on top of some papers, which she immediately tried to pull out from under him.

"Sailing? I don't have any clothes for that," she told him, thinking of her sparse wardrobe—and the fact that she'd never gone sailing before.

"You could come nude. It would be very interesting." His eyes sparkled as he ran his finger brazenly over her lips. They tingled at his touch, and Brittany felt as if she were unclothed already.

Embarrassed, she looked down at her work and began sorting the papers Blake wasn't sitting on. But he stopped her hands by catching them in his own and she felt him looking down at her.

"I'm not all that bad when you get to know me. Get to know me, Brittany." He said her name so softly and seriously that she had to look up. The next moment the light banter was back. "How about it? Just a harmless little sail on Lake Saguaro. Lots of people sail on the lake. Nothing will happen," he promised, holding up his hand solemnly.

She wanted to ask why he wasn't taking Sheila, but she also wanted to be with him so badly that the taunt died on her lips.

"I'll look silly dressed like this," she protested, hoping to be talked out of going. Her good sense told her she had lost her mind, but another part of her—the part that Blake had awakened with his kisses—urged her to throw caution to the winds.

"Oh, did I forget to tell you?" Blake asked innocently. "My father's taken care of your clothes." She looked at him, puzzled. "Why don't you just go upstairs and change?" he suggested.

"Alright," she agreed slowly, wary but curious. Blake followed her out of the library and up the stairs to her room where she went directly to the closets and threw open the doors. They were filled with clothes!

"Where did all this come from?" Brittany exclaimed, annoyed at this latest effort by the Kincade men to wear down her defenses. Instead of only five occupied hangers she now saw more than thirty filled with dresses, skirts, and blouses, all in her size. Beneath them stood a neat row of shoes in matching colors. This was her room, wasn't it? Yes, there were her brown, gray, and navy clothes all pushed to one side. Bewildered, Brittany turned to Blake, who was standing in the doorway.

"I told you my father has taken a shine to you," he said, leaning casually against the door frame.

"But I can't accept this," Brittany protested, "and I certainly can't pay for it. The dress was one thing, but this is outrageous!"

"You'd hurt his feelings if you—"

She pushed past Blake, not giving him a chance to finish, and hurried downstairs to the den, where she had last seen Ambroise. He was still there playing chess with Etienne, as was his custom after lunch.

She burst into the room, breathless from running. "Mr. Kincade, I am overwhelmed by your generosity," she began, "but—"

"Good, then wear the clothes in good health," he interrupted, waving her away as he studied the board.

"But—"

"Stop stammering," he interrupted again, finally glancing up with a dark scowl. "As long as you're going to be here, Britt, you're part of my household, and I won't have those gloomy clothes staring me in the face all the time. It's as if you're waiting for someone to die."

Brittany felt utterly frustrated and deeply touched. "I'm speechless," she said, and she was. No one had ever gone out of his way for her before. She turned to

Etienne, but his impassive face revealed nothing.

Ambroise nodded with approval. "Good, that's the way all women should be. Now get along and do whatever you were doing. Go for a walk, why don't you? It would do you good." He waved her away and went back to his chess game.

Brittany turned to go, then spun back around and impulsively kissed Ambroise's whiskered cheek. He smiled broadly. "Go on before I forget how old I am," he growled.

"Your move," Etienne prompted, as Brittany ran out of the room.

"No, it's Blake's, by heaven," she overheard Ambroise say. She didn't stop to consider what he might have meant.

Lake Saguaro was a manmade reservoir, peaceful and beautiful. Except for a few sailboats in the distance, there wasn't a soul around.

Brittany lay back in Blake's sailboat, basking in the hot sun. Despite the fact that she'd never been sailing before, she didn't feel at a disadvantage, as she usually did with Blake—partly because the bright terry-cloth robe she wore over her swimsuit made her feel chic and pretty. It amazed her to consider how much clothes could influence the way she felt about herself.

Idly she glanced around her. "I thought you said there'd be a lot of people here," she reminded Blake.

"There are—on weekends," he told her. "Right now, we've got most of the lake to ourselves."

He was wearing a tan shirt, open down the front, and swimming briefs. Brittany could easily see the fine layer of soft, dark hair that covered his chest, so fine that the hard muscles beneath were not hidden from view. His build was athletic, for he participated in many sports and worked out as well. His bathing suit hugged his hips, which were trim, and showed off his taut stomach. The

Greeks had built statues of their gods that looked just like Blake, Brittany thought, wondering if she had lost all her good sense by coming here with him. But so far he'd behaved himself, telling her about the lake and relating several stories of misadventures he'd had while sailing. He didn't seem to mind laughing at himself in the least. Slowly Brittany let down her guard.

Blake handled the sail expertly, and the easy breeze filled it gently. "Hey, I almost forgot," he said. "If we're going to go swimming, you'd better put this on." He fished some suntan lotion out of his pack of provisions.

"No, I—" Brittany began to protest, changing her mind about swimming. But Blake was already pulling the short terry-cloth robe off her shoulders. Under it she wore a one-piece white bathing suit that hugged her curves, outlining her perfect shape.

"That Etienne is a wonder," Blake said, eyeing the suit—and her—appreciatively. "Here, turn around." He began to apply the lotion ever so slowly, and Brittany began to feel as if she were getting a massage rather than having suntan lotion applied. Her skin began to tingle. Blake worked along the length of her legs, lingering about her thighs until she thought she would scream. His hand drifted toward the top of her shoulders, then worked its way down the plane of her throat and further to the top of her breasts.

"I think you'd better stop there," she said with effort, shooting him a warning look.

His hand brushed lightly against the top of her breasts. "I wouldn't want to see them sunburned," he said innocently.

"I'll take care of it, thank you," she said, grabbing the bottle from his hand.

"Well, now that you have the bottle, do me," he ordered, sitting down with his back toward her.

For a brief moment she gazed mesmerized at his back, at a loss how to begin. Then, squeezing a small amount of lotion into the palm of her hand, she began spreading it on his broad, muscular back as fast as she could. Her long fingers grazed him lightly, refusing to linger, for touching him did things to her she had only read about in books and seen in old movies.

"Hey, hey," Blake protested, laughing. "You're not greasing a pig here. Do it slowly. You wouldn't want to miss a spot and make me burn my delicate skin, would you?" he taunted.

"Your delicate skin has got the deepest tan I've ever seen," she retorted dryly, finishing the task with rapid motions.

"So you've noticed it—and have you noticed me?" he asked, turning around to tease her with his twinkling eyes and mischievous grin.

"You come on bigger than life, so it's a little difficult not to notice you," she replied, wishing she didn't feel so fluttery inside. "But don't let it go to your head."

"I believe in living life to the fullest," he told her simply in a more serious tone. "There might not be that much life left." He looked far away for a moment, leaving her wondering exactly what he'd meant, then his eyes focused on her again. "C'mon, let's dock the boat and go for a swim before the sun goes down. You wouldn't want to be with me on the lake after sundown, would you?" he added naughtily.

"Swimming's a very good idea," she replied, not really answering.

Blake pointed the boat toward shore and tied it securely to a bush, then turned to her, his eyes gliding warmly over her long and supple body. "Ready?" he asked, taking her hand.

"For what?" she asked, suspiciously eyeing the grin on his tanned face. The word sounded almost like a proposition.

Blake threw back his head and laughed. "For anything," he said and then ran, pulling her behind him

toward the water. He didn't have to pull long, as she
joined in his lighthearted mood and dove into the water.
It felt warm and wonderful as it licked her thighs and
sides, encompassing her in a velvety comfort. She swam
underwater, playfully hiding from Blake, only to have
him overtake her and pull her close to him.

Even beneath the surface, the thrill of feeling his body
next to hers awakened all her senses. She tried to tell
herself it was only the lack of air that made her feel so
heady, made her want to experience all the wonderful
things she had once dreamed were possible—all with a
man who was almost a stranger to her. No, that was
unfair. In the short time she had been with Blake, she
felt closer to him than she had ever felt to Jonathan,
despite the three years they had spent as man and wife.

Just then Blake took her into his arms and kissed her.
It was almost a tender kiss, but it stirred deep passions
within her that suddenly frightened her.

Brittany surfaced quickly, gasping for air. Blake
bobbed up right next to her, his eyes sparkling. "Women
are often breathless around me," he teased lightly, tread-
ing water with ease and overwhelming her with his nearness.

"Why?" she asked dryly. "Do you hold them all under
water like that?"

For an answer he only laughed and called out, "Tag,
you're it," like a small boy, and swam off.

The spirit of fun had returned, and Brittany tried to
match his powerful strokes, which she suspected he kept
slightly in check for her benefit. But she was a strong
swimmer herself, and she finally overtook and tagged
him.

He was after her like a shot. Laughing wholeheartedly,
she couldn't fully utilize her stroke, and consequently
Blake caught her within a few minutes, pulling her beneath the water by her foot. She brushed up against him,
hard, and the strap of her bathing suit slipped off in the

struggle. Too late she read the mischief in his eyes as he tugged on it further, exposing one ripe breast to his burning view.

Appalled, Brittany pulled up the wayward material, but his hand got in the way, covering her breast and shooting fire through her veins. She surfaced again, sputtering, her emotions warring within her. A man's touch had never done this to her. She had never wanted to be held and caressed by a man as she wanted to be held and caressed by Blake. But everything she had ever been taught told her that to give in to the casual pleasures he held out to her would be wrong. Giving in would only lead to heartbreak in the end.

"You shouldn't hide nature's perfect works of art from me like that," Blake said, but he pulled his hand away ever so slowly.

Brittany felt waves of heat playing on her skin, but she kept her face angry. "You look like you'd like to have me shot," Blake commented. Then his voice grew softer, "Would you?"

"I—I don't know what to say to you. You seem to think the whole world's your playground," she accused hotly.

"You'll come to know me better than that," he promised, his eyes whispering to her, urging her to give in.

"I think you're a little too familiar with me now," she retorted, playing on his words.

Blake only laughed, a warm, resonant sound. "C'mon," he told her. "I'll race you back."

With that, he turned his muscular back on her and gazed toward shore. "Unless, of course, you'd like to stay here and play in the water some more." The smile on his lips was whimsical as he cocked his dark head and glanced at her over his shoulder.

"Shore it is," Brittany said, beginning to swim back ahead of him.

The race was a relatively short one, but Brittany strove

hard to stay ahead of Blake, determined to beat him, determined not to be categorized with the other women he had known. She pushed to one side all the newly aroused yearnings that danced in her head, for she was afraid to explore them now, afraid because he was so near. Despite her show of annoyance, she felt vulnerable and uncertain. How could she keep resisting him?

Brittany made it to shore a scant second ahead of Blake and threw herself down on the towel he'd spread out, breathing hard. Blake joined her, lying down next to her. She eyed him critically. "You didn't let me win, did you?" she asked, seriously, propping herself up on one elbow.

"Would it bother you if I had?" he asked.

"I like to win on my own," she told him proudly, meaning it.

He lifted a lock of hair off her forehead. "Now you understand racing. The thrill of honest victory." He said the last sentence softly. "You know, even wet you're very pretty. I didn't think anyone looked pretty wet."

"I..." Brittany had no time to say anything, for his mouth was over hers, and his kiss sent her headlong into a wave of desire far more powerful than the real waves she had just swum through. He kissed her forehead, her eyes, her cheek, her throat, working his way down to her breasts, which strained against the thin material of her bathing suit, the nipples swollen and tender. Darts of heat and excitement shot through her, and she knew, somewhere far away in her mind, that she should stop him, stop him before it was too late. She didn't mean anything to him. She was just a diversion on a beautiful afternoon. But, once his, that would never be enough for her. With an overwhelming effort she caught and held his hand just as he was about to slip the strap of her bathing suit off her trembling shoulder.

"No," she breathed. "Blake, no."

"There's nothing wrong with this, Brittany," he murmured, and his protest was like another caress on her senses. "It's natural. Let it happen," he whispered against her throat.

"No." She pushed him away and sat bolt upright. "I won't *let* it happen. It can't be casual," she insisted. Already he was beginning to mean too much to her and the thought terrified her.

Blake sighed but kept his good temper with admirable control. "I could hire a three-piece band," he joked, "but they might distract us."

She met his intense gaze, studying the crooked smile she had grown to love in so short a time, watching it deepen the dimple in his cheek. She wanted to trace it with her finger, kiss it... She stopped herself. She couldn't take any more of this.

"Blake, I'd like to go home now," she said firmly.

"Alright," he replied, getting up. "Brittany, I'll never force you to do anything you don't want to." The words were serious, but his eyes danced as he looked down at her. "But you do want to," he told her as they returned to the boat.

The trip back was quiet. Night was falling, and Blake concentrated on guiding them across the lake to the marina on the other side. Brittany struggled with her thoughts and emotions. Had Blake been right? Did she really want to give up everything she'd ever been taught, everything she'd lived by, and make love to him? And worse, did she want to make love to him with no promise of commitment of any sort from him? She refused to listen to the voice that answered the questions within her.

Blake was gone for several days after that. Brittany assumed, ruefully, that since she had turned him down, he was occupied with Sheila, who looked as if she'd give him everything he wanted. Well, that was all right with her. Let them have each other, Brittany thought angrily. They belonged together—thoughtless jet-setters who didn't care how they hurt the people around them. With grim purpose she undertook her job with new vigor. If she concentrated, she only thought about Blake once an hour. But frequently she found herself looking up, hoping he'd be standing in her doorway. He never was.

Two weeks later she found out why.

"Another race?" she asked Etienne at dinner one evening. She kept her voice low because she didn't want Ambroise to hear. He was engaged in conversation with several men who had come to call on him. "Where?"

"California. He was due in this morning, but..." Etienne shrugged eloquently. Brittany surmised there was something he wasn't telling her. Etienne always seemed to know everything about the comings and goings of the household.

"Sheila's probably holding a victory party for him," Brittany commented with a tinge of bitterness. "The least he could have done was call—let his father know he was alright."

"The very least," Etienne echoed. Brittany suspected he sensed her own deep concern.

"Well, if you'll excuse me," she said, "I'm finally getting to the good part of Elizabeth's story. The pages are all sorted, and now I can read from the beginning." She rose and returned to the library with only a nod from Ambroise, who was acting particularly gruff and preoccupied.

Brittany worked until well past ten that night, then went to bed, falling into a fitful sleep. She dreamed of Blake, first in Sheila's arms, then in a terrible accident. Both images tormented her. She awoke with a start— and realized at once that she wasn't alone. In the darkness she sensed a presence in her room. Perhaps it was her dream. Still, she called out, "Who's there?"

"Shhh."

Blake! Dressed in a short-sleeved shirt and slacks, he was sitting on the sofa by the window, looking for all the world as if he had a perfect right to be there. She saw his face clearly in the moonlight. He looked tired and drawn—not at all his usual carefree self. She pulled up the sheet that she had cast off in her sleep.

"No, don't do that," he begged. "I've had a hard day and deserve a little treat. I've been watching you sleep."

"I'm sure Sheila gave you all the treats you could handle," Brittany snapped, turning crimson. "What are you doing here?"

He sighed deeply. "I don't know. I just felt I had to tell you something, and then you looked so nice, sleeping..."

"What? What did you want to tell me?" she asked when he didn't continue.

He came over and sat down next to her on the bed. Her pulse raced at his nearness, and she yearned to smooth away his fatigue and sadness. "I won," he said simply.

"Oh." It wasn't what she had hoped to hear.

"I'm sure glad the crowd at the track responded better than that," he commented wryly. He seemed to sway a little. She reached over to switch on the light on the night stand.

"Did you just get in?" she asked. This was absurd. She was carrying on a conversation in the middle of the night with her employer's son! She wasn't even dressed! Her light blue nightgown had lots of lace that revealed more than it concealed. She had found it tucked into her drawer, another Etienne "special."

Brittany grew self-conscious and angry. Blake hadn't even told her he was going to the race. Did he just expect to march into her room and have her melt in his arms like some quivering little fool?

"I arrived right this minute," Blake told her. "I flew to your side with the good news, so to speak. Mind if I lie down for a minute?"

"Yes, I do mind," she said, annoyed at his casual manner.

"That's no way to treat a winner," Blake told her, disregarding her words and lying down full length on the bed. She was sure he was going to reach for her at any moment, and half of her anticipated the contact of his hand on her. But it never happened.

He was out cold. She regarded him in surprise, wondering what was wrong. Gingerly she tried to nudge him, but he couldn't be roused. Sudden alarm shot through her. She threw on her robe and ran out of the room in search of Etienne.

"Post concussion syndrome," the doctor told Ambroise some time later as he sat, concerned, in Blake's room with Brittany and Etienne standing behind him. They had summoned Ambroise's private doctor immediately. "He'll be all right in the morning. Just see to it that he gets plenty of rest—and stays out of race cars for a little while."

Ambroise nodded, following the man out. "Even if we have to tie him down," he vowed.

"Hey, I'm not dead yet," Blake scolded. "Don't hold the wake." He had awakened some time ago and now sat propped up in bed, scowling darkly at Brittany and Etienne, reminding her strongly of her first encounter with Ambroise.

"What happened?" Brittany demanded when Etienne just continued frowning in silence.

"I hit my head in the practice run. The car spun out, but I regained control. I won, didn't I?"

"This time," Brittany spat, furious with him. "How much longer are you going to tempt fate?" she demanded. His recklessness appalled her.

"Until I get it right, Sacajawea," he said, idly smoothing the sheet about his waist as he leaned against three pillows. "Now lower your voice in respect for the walloping headache I have."

"I see you're back to your old self," Etienne commented. "I shall see you in the morning." He rose to leave.

"Right," Blake said. "Take the edge off the old man for me, will you?" He winked.

"I'll do what I can," Etienne promised dryly as he closed the door behind him.

Brittany was angry and didn't know how to hide it. After all, it was Blake's neck—and her heart, she thought ruefully. She looked about the room, trying to think of something to say. It was a large, comfortable room with little furniture except Blake's bed, dresser, and desk. On the far wall hung tropies and plaques from his races. Brittany couldn't bear to look at them.

Her eyes stopped at a framed picture of a woman on the bureau. Another girlfriend, she thought, and then her eyes narrowed a little. The woman actually looked like her, but upon closer scrutiny she realized that, of course, it wasn't her. The face was rounder and the hair was worn differently, shorter. Brittany was reaching out to pick it up for a closer look when Blake's voice, deathly still, stopped her.

"Don't touch that," he said, and she drew back her hand. "Sorry, temporary loss of good manners," he apologized. "That's Anne."

Brittany turned away, unaccountably hurt because he didn't want to share more with her, but willing to respect his privacy. Not only did she have living rivals, but there was his late wife as well.

"I'd better go," she said.

Blake's expression changed. "Stay awhile," he pleaded. "I said I was sorry."

"You *should* be sorry," she said, her voice rising. "That was a stupid thing you did. Why don't you stop racing before you kill yourself?"

"I've got a few more races before the season's over and then we'll see," he told her.

"You're impossible," she said angrily.

"I've been told that." He caught her hand as she turned to leave. "Stay. I'm afraid of the dark," he teased. She sat down on the edge of the bed. "Talk to me," he said. "Fill the room with words. What's been happening here in the past two weeks? What's your favorite flower? Do you like strays?"

She laughed at his questions and began telling him what he wanted to know. By the time she had told him that, yes, she had had a stray puppy once and her favorite flowers were roses, he appeared to have fallen asleep.

Brittany gazed down at his face, almost boyish in sleep, with no banter, no guard up against the world. She brushed back a lock of hair that had fallen across his forehead. Then, giving in to an urge, she lightly kissed his forehead—and suddenly found herself pulled closer, a burning kiss planted on her surprised lips.

"Caught you." Blake laughed, although a little weakly.

Brittany was upset and annoyed at having let her guard down so completely. She didn't want him to think of her the way he did all the other women he knew. Abruptly, she freed herself.

"I'm not caught. Not by a long shot," she lied. And with that, she left the room.

The next day Sheila arrived, full of oohs and aahs and sympathy, sailing into Blake's room with an armload of flowers.

"I was just devastated when Etienne said you weren't well enough to be disturbed," she said, rudely elbowing Brittany away from the bed. "I'll be your nurse, darling, and take good care of you," she purred, arranging his pillow for him. "Get a vase for these flowers," she told Brittany, who stiffened, clenching her fists at her sides.

"I'll get someone who's paid to fetch it for you," she

replied frostily, and left the room before Blake could stop her.

"Well, that gets rid of her at any rate," she heard Sheila say loftily. She didn't catch Blake's response as she ran down the stairs to the library.

chapter

5

BLAKE WAS UP and about within a day, but Brittany kept out of his way, engrossing herself in her work. Ambroise had found a picture of his great-grandmother, which made the story of Elizabeth's life and trials all the more vivid.

Elizabeth McCandles had been a small girl with thick blond braids and an innocent face. The picture was dated 1868, so it must have been taken shortly before she was abducted.

Brittany read with absorbed interest about the way Nachise had immediately chosen Elizabeth as his property, saving her from the humiliation of being violated by all the braves. Brittany wondered how she herself would have reacted in a situation like that and shivered with dread. She continued reading a section Elizabeth had written many years later, looking back at the incident.

The popular thought of the day said it was better to kill yourself than let the enemy lay hands on you. But those words were uttered by ladies in parlors who let their imaginations run wild. I could not willingly accept death. Life was too dear, too precious, and I hung on at all costs. My unhappiness decreased as time wore on. Nachise was gentle in his own way. I was surprised. Perhaps having three wives before me taught him kindness, although his wives were anything but kind to me. Still, I survived. There is no shame in surviving.

The words were hard to read in places, time having marred the pages and faded the ink, but Brittany pressed on, so intrigued that she forgot to transcribe. She decided to read the manuscript through once from beginning to end before writing it down.

Despite his other worries and responsibilities, Ambroise demanded from her a verbal summary of the day's reading each evening. It was the only way he would allow Brittany to read the journal first without him. It became her habit to come to him an hour before dinner. One evening, a week after Blake's accident, she had just finished such a session when Blake entered his father's den.

"Are you through with today's inquisition?" he asked his father, nodding toward Brittany.

"I enjoy this," she protested. "It keeps events fresh in my mind." She hadn't talked to Blake since the incident in his room with Sheila, but her anger with him, as well as her desire, glowed like a hot ember just beneath her calm surface.

"Good, you can tell me the story over dinner," Blake said. "I need to get out, and I want you to go with me."

"I have work to do," she said coldly, rising. "Why don't you ask Sheila?"

As if Ambroise wasn't even in the room, Blake took hold of her arm a little roughly, which surprised her. He had always been gentle with her before. Immediately he lessened the intensity of his grip. "If I wanted Sheila," he said with an ease that belied his firm grip, "I would have asked her. Now, as the boss's son, I order you to come to dinner with me."

Brittany looked toward Ambroise for help, but she

should have known better than to expect it from the gruff old gentleman, who seemed to encourage his son's pursuit at every opportunity. "Better do as he says, Britt," he told her, hiding a half-smile, "or he's apt to get violent."

She knew Ambroise was joking, but she also knew she didn't want to be alone with Blake. Her week away from him hadn't made her any less vulnerable to his touch.

"I promise to behave," Blake added with an engaging grin. "Boy scout's honor. Besides, would you have me waste these tickets?"

From his jacket pocket he produced two theater tickets for *Oklahoma!* at the Civic Center in Phoenix.

"Box seats," Brittany read with longing. Except for amateur church plays she had never seen a theatrical performance. Her eyes lit up with excitement.

"Only the best for our historian," Blake told her, obviously pleased with her enthusiasm. "Now, is it a deal or do I go to my room and sulk?"

Tempted beyond restraint, Brittany decided impulsively to take another chance. "Give me half an hour," she told him, racing from the room.

"Beauty, charm, brains, and fast, too," she heard Ambroise say behind her with a laugh.

Less clearly she heard Blake reply, "Only in certain ways, dad. Only in certain ways."

A wide smile came to Brittany's lips as she hurried to get ready, stripping off her clothes and stepping into the shower. Perhaps...just perhaps, she was finally getting to Blake after all. The thought brought an excited sparkle to her eyes and hope to her heart.

Exactly thirty-five minutes later Blake pulled up in front of the house in an XKE sports car. "Do I get into that or just straddle it?" Brittany asked, half-serious, half-teasing.

"Madam, you are insulting one of my prized possessions," Blake retorted with mock chagrin. "This is vintage 1967 and I take loving care of it. Here, let me help." He held her arm for balance as she lowered herself into the seat and tucked her dress inside the cramped interior. Her evening dress was accented with thin straps that tied provocatively on her shoulders. The empire bodice accentuated the firm lift of her breasts, and the skirt hinted softly at the sway of her hips as she walked.

"Has anyone ever told you you've got lovely legs?" Blake asked, smiling at her with warm intimacy.

"No one's ever told me I've got a lovely anything," she said, then bit her tongue at her poor choice of words.

"Then your husband was a fool," Blake told her with a hint of anger. "If I'd been him, I would have taken inventory every day and told you how lovely it all was." He came around to the driver's side and slid into the seat beside her.

"This is like sitting in a ladle," Brittany told him as she stretched out her legs before her and studied the complex instrument panel.

"One fast ladle," Blake agreed, opening up the throttle just a little, which catapulted them down the road in a silver streak. Brittany held onto the seat for dear life.

"Can trucks see us?" she asked as they headed down the highway toward the center of Phoenix.

"We're not whizzing by that fast," Blake protested, laughing.

"No, I mean we're so close to the ground," she explained, "and they're so high up. It almost seems we could slip right under one of those semitrailer trucks."

Blake threw back his head and laughed, the deep, resonate sound filling the car and making Brittany feel safe and warm, despite her feeling that she should be angry with him for laughing at her. "Don't worry. I'll get us there in one piece."

A fairly strong breeze was coming through a crack

in the car window, and she lifted her hair, trapping it against the head rest as she leaned back to keep it from blowing around. Suddenly the coolness was shattered as she felt Blake's fingers glide gently along the back of her neck, stroking it softly. A wave of warmth engulfed her. Without realizing it she sighed, remembering what it was like to be in his arms.

"Don't you think you should use two hands?" she asked, her eyes indicating the steering wheel.

"I'd love to," he told her, "but I need one for driving."

She scowled up at him, pretending to be more annoyed with him than she really felt, with his hand still stroking her hair. "That line is as old as the hills."

"So's this feeling inside." To her surprise, he almost sounded sincere, and her heart seemed to do a little flip inside her.

Brittany wet her lips. "You're unbelievable, you know that? Where are we going?" she asked, changing the subject. Why was he doing this to her? And why had she come? It was torture being with him, fighting the temptation he offered, wondering what he really felt for Sheila and what the extent of his commitment to her was, yet painfully unable to ask the question that would either open the floodgates of hope or destroy forever her secret dreams and longings.

"The agenda calls for a light dinner," Blake was saying, "then the show at the Civic Center, then a little dancing, et cetera, et cetera." He looked over at her, his eyes shining.

"Sounds nice, but cancel the 'et cetera,'" Brittany told him, back to her prim and proper self.

"But that's the best part."

"Blake . . ." Her voice went up a warning note.

"Shh, we're here."

He got out of the car and went around to open her door. Brittany emerged with some effort and stumbled slightly. He caught her instantly in his arms, pulling her closer to him than was necessary. Drawn to him in spite of everything, she couldn't help meeting his intense gaze.

"Well, if you'd like to start with the et cetera now . . ." he began huskily.

She shook her head, her mind in a daze, then immediately recollected herself. "Walk," she ordered, laughing. "I'm hungry."

"So am I," he whispered into her hair. The shiver that went through her wasn't caused by the cool night air. Gallantly Blake presented his arm to her, and together they walked into the elegant restaurant.

The maitre d' recognized Blake immediately. Naturally, Brittany thought. As she watched Blake speak to the man, she couldn't help noticing how dashing her escort looked. He was dressed in a custom-tailored, pearl-gray suit with a blue-gray shirt that set off his eyes—as if they needed setting off. His eyes weaved their magic with no help whatsoever. Brittany was beginning to think she was bewitched.

They were seated right away at one of the better tables, while people who had come ahead of them still stood waiting in line. The restaurant was dimly lit. A single candle flickered in a glass bowl on their table, casting a romantic glow.

"Money certainly does speak," Brittany whispered to Blake, glancing at the line they had passed so easily.

"And it says the nicest things. It brought you into my life, didn't it?" he asked as he took the wine list from the waiter, who appeared almost magically at his elbow, welcoming him with a smile.

"How so?" she asked, not understanding the connection.

"If my father weren't rich and slightly bored, he could never have indulged himself in this 'roots' odyssey of his and hired you."

"You don't think very much of this project, do you?" she asked.

He shrugged and indicated his choice of wine to the waiter.

"Excellent," the waiter murmured. He would have murmured "excellent" if Blake had ordered rubbing alcohol, Brittany thought, amused.

"But Elizabeth is your relation, too," she protested, not understanding Blake's detachment.

He toyed with his water glass, twirling it around on its stem. "She's someone who lived and died in the past. She has no bearing on today."

"If she had no 'bearing,'" Brittany said, seizing on the word, "you wouldn't be here—"

"—enjoying your company," he interrupted, his hand closing over hers.

"I enjoy reading about the past," she persisted, trying to make her point. She felt he was teasing her, testing her to see what she was made of.

Blake's face sombered just a little and his jaw tightened. "The past is gone," he said. "You can't get it back and it doesn't keep you warm at night. The present is all that counts."

"The present isn't isolated. It's part of a network. You learn from the past." She lowered her voice as the waiter returned with the wine.

The man presented a small sample to Blake and, at Blake's nod of approval, poured two glasses. Only when the man left did Blake even look as if he had heard any part of her last statement. He studied his wine glass before answering.

"Perhaps you do learn. You learn not to grow attached to anything because it won't stay."

The momentary look of hurt in his eyes made Brittany want to reach out to him, to hold him, to make his pain disappear. This time she pressed his hand without even thinking. The cloud over his eyes passed.

"I'm sorry about your wife," she ventured softly.

He looked a bit surprised at her words. "So am I,"

he said quietly. His eyes looked off into the distance, not quite seeing anything. "She was a warm and wonderful person. Seeing life through her eyes, I could almost believe that there was good in everything around me."

"How long did you know her?" Brittany asked, feeling as if she were intruding, yet needing very much to know.

"Not nearly long enough," he told her. His face brightened a little. "And what about you?" he asked.

"What about me?" she echoed, surprised at his sudden change of topic.

"What about your husband?" Blake prodded. "I really know very little about your past."

Brittany toyed with her drink, a small smile on her lips. "Perhaps it's better that way." She raised her eyes to look at him. "You know, I'll be a woman of intrigue . . ."

"Oh no, you don't get off that easily." He laughed, shifting his hand under hers and running his thumb along her palm. "You can't peek into my soul and then pull back, expecting to get away scot-free." His expression turned serious for a moment. "Was it a love match?"

Brittany thought she was going to choke as she shook her blond head. "Hardly. I suppose you could say I just drifted into it."

"You don't strike me as a drifter," Blake replied.

She shrugged her slim shoulders. "My father approved highly of Jonathan. He was a minister, as well, and my father thought it was a good match. Certainly Jonathan was a good man," she added in a detached voice. "And I was realistic enough to know that the prince of my dreams had left his charger double-parked somewhere and wasn't about to ride into my life and sweep me off my feet."

"And so you got married?" Blake asked incredulously. "Did you even like him?"

"Oh, I liked him alright. He was a comfortable man

and very kind to his flock," she said with a smile.

"How was he to his wife?" Blake asked, leaning forward.

She smiled ruefully. "A bit forgetful. He was ten years older than I was and much more set in his ways. He thought I was a bit frivolous, but he forgave me." Her voice held a touch of amusement. "It really wasn't as bad as it sounds," she added suddenly, realizing what Blake must be thinking. "My marriage was the way most marriages should be—about twenty years down the road," she added with a small sigh. "I really shouldn't be telling you all this."

"Why not?" Blake wanted to know.

"Because it's private—and boring, and you've got much more exciting things to do than to listen to the capsulized life of a minister's daughter," she said, shifting self-consciously in her seat. His eyes never left her face.

"I can't think of anything else I'd rather be doing—except maybe one," he said wickedly. "And nothing about you is boring, Sacajawea." He raised his glass and waited until she followed suit. "Alright, no more talk about the past. To tonight, Sacajawea, and to you," he said, toasting her. And then he laughed as she gazed down, embarrassed at his attention and at the way she had confided in him about her private life. "You've got the most adorable blush, Sacajawea. It's hard to believe you're even part of this mad world of ours."

"I'm not," she said with a smile, sipping her wine and feeling the warmth all the way down to her stomach. "I'm a throwback."

"I could really believe that," he told her, laughing. But his smile was far from mocking. It almost sounded like a compliment, Brittany thought as she looked down at her menu.

They ordered. No sooner had the meal arrived than

a well-dressed young woman in a tight-fitting dress appeared at their table, her eyes full of delight at seeing Blake.

"Blake, you beast, why haven't you called me?" she asked after kissing him soundly. A diamond necklace gleamed at her throat, and gold bracelets flashed on her wrists. Brittany felt suddenly out of her element.

"You know how things get, Pamela," Blake said, smiling. "I'd like you to meet—"

"I saw you race last week," Pamela interrupted, placing her hand on his shoulder. "You devil, you've taken up with Sheila, and she doesn't have a thing I don't have more of." Pamela glanced over at Brittany, then turned a smug face back to Blake. "Let me know when you want to get back into the big league," she said, then sauntered off, her hips swaying provocatively.

"When he's in a pitching slump," Brittany said after her, loud enough to make Blake laugh.

"You've got a temper there," he commented. "Don't worry. She's just an old friend."

"Uh-huh." Her tone was skeptical.

"Sacajawea, I'm not exactly a monk," Blake admitted, holding her gaze.

"More like a sultan," she corrected.

"Want to see the harem quarters?" he bantered.

"Wouldn't it be too crowded?" she asked, pretending to be very interested in her sautéed scallops. Despite his casual tone—or maybe because he was treating so lightly something she considered very serious—Brittany found it impossible to join his game wholeheartedly.

"I'm sure we could find a place for you to lie down," he said, his eyes dancing merrily.

She went on eating, not replying.

"Hey," he said, grabbing her right hand, "why are you rushing? Didn't your mother teach you to chew your food?" he asked.

"We'll be late for the show," she said, having just realized what time it was.

"Fashionably late," he corrected her.

"I don't want to be late, fashionably or otherwise. I want to see every bit of it." She looked as delighted with the prospect as an innocent child.

Blake leaned his head against his hand and studied her intently. "You are refreshing, Sacajawea, you really are."

"Not like Sheila?" she couldn't help asking. The words came out before she could stop them.

He raised a brow, then let it drop. "Not like anyone I've ever met," he said softly, still watching her.

They arrived at the theater just in time. The house lights had just begun to dim as they groped their way to their reserved seats. Taking her seat high above the stage, Brittany was dazzled by the ultramodern theater filled with people and the colorful stage sets below. She felt she'd entered another world.

The curtain went up on the Civic Center's revival of *Oklahoma!*, and for the next two and a half hours Brittany sat entranced by beautiful music, ingenious sets, and a kind of magic that delighted her soul. Blake had taken her hand during the performance, and it seemed to fit within his as if God had created it for just that purpose. "Make this moment last forever," she prayed silently. "Let it never, ever end." She glanced at his profile once and thought how beautiful it was—his strong chin, his high cheekbones, his noble brow. She smiled to herself, thinking that she sounded as if she were trying to describe the romanticized prototype of the American Indian.

Blake caught her looking at him and smiled warmly, melting her heart before she turned away, embarrassed. He leaned forward, his breath tickling her neck as he whispered, "Take notes, now."

In a second she realized what he meant. Ado Annie was singing, "I'm Just a Girl Who Can't Say No."

It was all Brittany could do to hide the smile that sprang to her lips. Blake was always in there, trying. And had circumstances been different, she might have let him. But there were all his former girlfriends and Sheila and the ghost of his dead wife—terrible odds for someone who didn't even know how to play poker and bluff her way, she thought sadly.

At one point the stage grew dark as stagehands shifted scenery for the next act. All of a sudden Blake leaned over and began kissing her with an urgency that took her breath away. She pulled back nervously.

"People will see us," she whispered fiercely.

"Only if they have X-ray vision," he assured her. "I see my opportunities and I take them." He moved to kiss her again, but she eluded his grasp.

A game. It was just a game to him, she tried to remind herself. But in the darkness she ran her fingers over her lips, as if to seal in his kiss and preserve the moment.

As the stage lightened, Blake saw her hastily put down her hand, and she caught his smile. For the duration of the play he seemed to watch her more than he did the stage. She found his attention disconcerting, but for some reason it heightened rather than detracted from her enjoyment of the play.

"Want to go backstage?" he asked when it was over.

"Can we?" she asked, enchanted with the idea.

"Sure. I know Adam Nelson, the star," he told her matter-of-factly.

She shook her head. "Who don't you know?" She shivered as he placed her wrap about her shoulders, letting his fingers linger on her bare skin.

"You," he whispered huskily in her ear before leading her out.

Still tingling, Brittany let the subject drop.

Moving slowly through the departing crowds, Brittany was awed by the glamorously dressed men and women around her. Yet Blake was so possessive of her, so solicitous of her comfort and enjoyment, that she felt every bit as beautiful as they were.

The backstage area was noisy and alive with people — actors and actresses still in their costumes, as well as enthusiastic visitors dressed in street clothes. Everyone bustled about with enviable energy, making Brittany feel like a pebble tossed about in a great sea.

Finally she and Blake arrived at Adam Nelson's dresssing room, which was packed with what appeared to be almost half the cast. They fought their way to the actor's side, Blake greeting several acquaintances along the way — most of them women, Brittany noted ruefully. The star welcomed Blake with a shouted, "Well, look who finally showed up!" and a huge hug. To Brittany's surprise he actually seemed relieved to see them. He acknowledged Blake's hasty introduction with an awkward handshake in the cramped quarters and immediately suggested they leave.

"Listen, there's a club a couple of blocks from the theater," he told them. "Why don't we go there for a few drinks? We can talk, and I can unwind. And maybe steal your girl," he added, winking at Brittany.

Blake's girl. She liked the sound of that, liked being paired. But her irrepressible honesty caused her to put the lie to rest. "I'm really not Blake's girl," she said. "Just a friend."

"All the better for me," Adam replied jovially.

But Blake put his arm possessively around her shoulders. "I think, old buddy, you'd better take your co-star with you, unless you want to be lonely," he told him in a friendly voice.

Brittany looked up at Blake in surprise. Did he care, just a little? Was he jealous of the attention Adam was

paying her? Or was it just that he didn't like anyone
taking his toys away from him before he was finished
playing with them?

"That's okay, Mavis is crazy about me," Adam told
them.

Within half an hour the foursome was sitting in a club
frequented by people looking for a good time, which
they seemed to equate with the volume of noise they and
the band could make. Brittany had trouble hearing herself
think—although she knew by now what all her thoughts
were about anyway. No matter what the conversation,
and what she could hear of it was entertaining, her
thoughts inevitably returned to Blake.

Brittany danced twice with Adam and once with
Blake. All three times it was almost impossible to move
amid the hordes of people all dancing wildly to the powerful beat.

After a while Brittany began to feel as if her head
were spinning away from her. Thirsty from all the ac-
tivity, she had drained her first glass of white wine a
little too quickly, and when Adam insisted on buying
another round, he wouldn't let her refuse. Partly in
words, partly in sign language, he ordered her to drink
up.

"Want another?" Blake asked an hour later, shouting
into her ear.

Brittany moved her head closer to hear and the smell
of his skin made her heart pound faster. She could swear
he kissed her forehead ever so lightly.

"I don't think so," she shouted back.

"Fine," Blake replied and ordered a third drink for
her.

She took it without thinking, feeling somewhat giddy.
Another new experience, she thought as her mental state
went to a lighter, airier plane.

When she was finished, Blake studied her closely and
apparently decided it was time to leave.

"C'mon," he said, taking her hand and grabbing up her purse for her. "It's getting too crowded. I know a place where it's nice and quiet, and there's music so we can dance slowly."

"That sounds nice," Brittany shouted.

She waved good night to Adam and Mavis and found herself sitting in Blake's XKE before she knew it.

"You may have to carry me out of this thing," she told him, giggling. "I think my legs are falling asleep. When does the rushing noise stop?" she added, touching her ears.

"It was a little loud, wasn't it?" Blake admitted.

"There were more people in that club than in the town I came from," Brittany told him and laughed again at her own statement. She certainly had come a long way in a short time.

What seemed like hours later, she realized that the car had stopped moving. "Where are we?" she asked, peering out the window at what appeared to be a row of expensive-looking town houses, each different from the other.

Blake helped her out of the car and, indeed, Brittany almost had to be lifted out. But Blake seemed in no hurry to let go of her once she was standing firmly on the sidewalk.

She looked past his shoulder at the impressive exterior of the building that a sign indicated was the Arizona Biltmore Hotel. Blake told her it had been designed by Frank Lloyd Wright. Her eyes returned to his face. "What are we doing here?" she asked suspiciously.

"I thought you might like to get away from the madding crowd," he said, leading her past a doorman, who nodded hello and tipped his hat in recognition.

Words of protest did not seem to materialize past Brittany's lips as she was ushered into a plush elevator and taken up to the fourth floor. Blake's suite of rooms was just down the hall. She felt as if she were walking through a dream. This wasn't really happening to her.

She had the strangest sensation of being separated from her body, the effect of the alcohol on her untrained stomach, she decided vaguely. Or did this feeling have another cause as well?

"You have a suite?" she asked, finding her voice at last.

"I stay here sometimes to get away from dad's nagging. At other times he uses this place to entertain certain guests he'd rather not have at the house." He unlocked and opened the door for her.

"The house being so crowded and all." She laughed, and he joined in. It was nice, laughing with him.

Brittany walked into a large, lavishly decorated living room. The modern decor made it look almost set apart from the rest of the world. The wallpaper was a muted gold leaf. Glass doors led to a balcony at the far end, which overlooked the heart of the city.

Blake closed the front door behind him and turned a switch on the wall. Suddenly the room was filled with the sound of violins as a romantic melody encompassed Brittany. She looked up toward the ceiling.

"Magic?" she inquired with a smile.

"Piped-in music," he told her, holding out his hands. "May I have this dance, madam?"

She glided into his arms like a lavender cloud.

His arms went around her, and she rested her head against his chest. How naturral it felt. If only there were no one else in the world but her and Blake.

The song ended and another began. They kept on dancing, twirling slowly about the room until Brittany felt quite dizzy. But still she didn't want to stop. It felt so good to be wrapped in Blake's strong arms, his hard chest pressing against her breasts, his long legs brushing her thighs through the thin material of her dress. It felt so idyllic, so perfect. She didn't want anything to spoil it—and she knew it would be spoiled if either one of them said anything.

Finally Blake slowed to a stop. He loosened his hold on her just enough to take off his jacket and tie and open the first two buttons of his shirt. "Ah, I can breathe again," he said. "Whoever invented ties certainly had it in for his fellow man. Useless appendages. Better suited for lynching." He sat down, patting the place next to him on the large blue sofa.

Gingerly Brittany sat down on the edge, the effects of the three drinks suddenly all gone.

"You look like you're ready to jump," he told her, laughing. "Relax. Take it easy. I never bite—unless asked to. Can I get you anything?"

"A taxi," she replied. "I shouldn't be here."

"Sure you should," he said, his voice soothing as he put his hand on her shoulder.

She moved away from his touch and stood up. "What about Sheila?"

Blake sighed. "You have the strangest way of ruining a conversation. Well, what about Sheila?" he asked.

"She's the one who should be here," Brittany said, heading for the balcony. She needed some air.

He followed, sounding annoyed. "What are you doing, running a campaign for Sheila? She's a big girl and can certainly further her own cause without you in there pitching for her."

"I'm not pitching for her," she retorted bitterly. "I don't have to."

"What's that supposed to mean?" Immediately he regained his good humor. "You've been working too hard, Brittany. You're beginning to sound like a mysterious Indian."

"Indians aren't mysterious," she disagreed. "They're just different from us. As to my meaning, Sheila seems to think she's engaged to you." Immediately she turned her back to him, wanting to kick herself. Once again her wayward tongue had gotten the best of her. She'd finally said the words she'd been afraid to say for weeks.

At first Blake appeared flabbergasted, then he simply shrugged. "Well, she's the only one who does think we're engaged."

Was he lying to her? Brittany wondered desperately. Could he possibly be telling her the truth?

"But that ring on her finger—"

"—was a trinket she liked," he finished, "so I got it for her. When you're rich, you can afford to be stupid sometimes. I never told her it was an engagement ring. When I get engaged, Sacajawea, I promise I'll know it. And it won't be something I'll try to hide. Now come down off your high horse and join me. In case you haven't noticed, it's rather lonely if we're not talking to one another."

Blake had been standing behind her. Now he reached out and touched her hair gently. She turned to look at him.

"Remember the last time we took in a view like this?" he asked softly, his hand gliding lightly along the bare expanse of her back and shoulders. He touched her skin softly, sending shivers down to her toes.

"Yes," she answered in a voice so quiet she hardly heard herself. She felt so warm, so pliant. She was fighting herself harder than she was fighting him. "You said you'd be good—boy scout's honor," she reminded him with effort.

"I flunked my scout's test," he replied teasingly, nibbling on her ear.

"You tried to get me drunk tonight to seduce me," Brittany accused him, suddenly realizing how the whole evening had gone.

"Oh, Brittany, what am I going to do with you?" Blake said, chuckling. And then he took her into his arms and kissed her with a fierceness that almost frightened her. Brittany's breath grew ragged as his lips caressed hers, his tongue sliding over hers, entwining with it, filling her with a sweet, melting ecstasy. She fought for control as her reserve crumbled to nothing.

Blake paused to catch his own breath. His eyes caressed her gently, making love to her all on their own. Her body tingled with anticipation while her mind struggled mightily to regain control.

"You keep wearing those inviting little straps," he said, slipping one off her shoulder. She grabbed for it and pulled it back. "Why do you wear them if you don't want me to slip them off?" he asked, still teasing.

"I like the dress," she said, using the first excuse that came to mind. Why *had* she worn the dress? another part of her demanded. "It's beautiful," she insisted.

"The dress is pretty. *You* are beautiful," he corrected. His eyes were no longer mischievous, no longer teasing. She read desire there and a need to have her that frightened her. "And the headiest drink I've ever pressed my lips to," he told her, taking hold of her again and kissing her in a way she had never been kissed before, even by him. Waves of swirling heat intoxicated her, whipping away her senses and uncovering deep wells of passion within her she had never dreamed existed.

Brittany pushed her hands feebly against his chest in a last effort to save herself, but he only pulled her closer, crushing her against him. She felt totally consumed by him, by the power of his demanding desire. Vaguely she realized he had picked her up in his arms, his lips never leaving hers, and was carrying her to the next room, then tenderly placing her on a bed. Blake was leaning over her before she could voice her protest.

He covered her with kisses, setting her entire body aflame. His lips brushed her hair, her throat, her shoulders, while his hands enveloped her, touching her, making her his. Somehow his hand slipped behind her and unzipped her dress in a fluid motion. As she moved, she felt it suddenly float away from her body, to be replaced by the feel of his burning hands upon her skin. The lacey strapless bra parted, leaving her breasts free to be gently nudged by his hand. He caressed her breasts possessively, first with his hands, then with his lips, which kissed a path between them. His tongue teasingly touched first one peaked nipple and then the other, as if savoring the effect.

Brittany arched her back against him as a moan escaped her lips. Her thoughts and feelings were in violent turmoil, pulling her in opposite directions, confusing and frustrating her until she wanted to scream. Tears sprang to her eyes as her yearning to be held and to be made love to fought with an entrenched sense of right and wrong that had been so deeply instilled in her.

Feeling her tears, Blake paused and looked down at her, his expression filling with concern. Abruptly he muttered an oath and sprang away from her to sit on the edge of the bed. Anger smoldered in his eyes. "Brittany, why are you crying? Why won't you give in to your feelings and let me make love to you? Brittany, I'm only human and you are so tempting." With a great deal of effort he seemed to pull himself together, his anger slowly fading as he stroked her hair absently. "Someday, someway, you're going to be mine, Brittany," he finally promised. "It's just a matter of time." And with that he walked out of the room.

Brittany sat up on the bed and began pulling her clothes back on, hot tears spilling freely down her cheeks. How could she love anyone who made her cry so much? There, she had admitted it to herself. She was in love with Blake, in love with a playboy who refused to make a commitment. How could this have happened to her?

She looked up and found Blake standing next to her. He handed her a tissue and sat down on the edge of the bed, keeping a safe distance between them. "Here, use this and stop crying. You look like Rudolph the Reindeer with that red nose."

She had to smile at his words.

"Feel better?" he asked.

She nodded.

"Good." Taking her hand, he helped her up. "Let's go home."

In silence they left the apartment. In silence they drove home, finally pulling into the dimly lighted courtyard of the Kincade home. Blake escorted Brittany to her bedroom door, kissed her lightly on the lips, and whispered, "Not tonight, Brittany, but someday, someday."

She stared down the hall long after he had disappeared into his own room, feeling strangely empty of all emotion.

The next day Brittany found she couldn't keep her mind on her work, even though she had started it early in the morning. Unaccountably restless, she wandered outside to the large, tear-shaped pool. She was all alone and glad of it. Sighing, she sat down by the poolside and stared into the water. Perhaps she should quit her job and leave . . . But there was Mr. Kincade to think of as well as herself. He expected her to finish the project, and, besides, Elizabeth McCandles's journal was as much her project now as it was his. She felt she had to see it through. But if she stayed, how long would it be before Blake succeeded in breaking through her thin resistance? Would he just go on to someone else? Probably. The only reason he came back to her now was the fact that she said no. If she said yes, the way her soul begged her to do, he would be gone with the dawn's light, a small present left in his wake. She couldn't bear that. She . . .

"You skipped breakfast."

Brittany jumped, not having heard him come up behind her.

"Hey, steady," Blake said. "The sound of my voice isn't supposed to scare you to death." He put his hand on her shoulder to keep her seated. He looked so tall, standing over her, so good-looking as he peeled off his T-shirt, exposing navy swim briefs that hugged his hips like a second skin. She pretended not to be aware of his magnificent physique as she stared down at the water.

"I wasn't hungry," she murmured in belated response to his comment.

"You've got to maintain your strength if you're going to keep fighting me off," he joked, then walked to the far end of the pool. He climbed onto the diving board, paused briefly, and executed a perfect dive. A young god. The words flashed through her mind.

"From Mr. Blake," said a voice at her elbow.

She turned to find one of the butlers holding a tray containing cheese and eggs, done the way she liked them, orange juice, and a single pink rose. Blake had remembered she liked roses.

She lifted the glass of orange juice in a mock toast to Blake, who swam over to her and emerged from the pool practically at her feet.

"I wouldn't want to take unfair advantage of you the next time," he teased.

There wouldn't be a next time, Brittany promised herself silently. But she knew inside she was lying to herself.

"I've been invited to a party at the home of one of my friends," Blake continued. "I already promised him I'd come weeks ago. It's tomorrow afternoon."

Brittany put down the glass of juice and watched Blake towel himself dry. "Why are you telling me all this?"

He leaned over to lift her chin in his hand and look deeply into her almond-shaped eyes. "Because you're going with me."

"Oh, no, I'm not," she said firmly, shaking her head and drawing away.

"I've already arranged for you to be sprung from jail," Blake went on, ignoring her protest. "Your warden has given you the afternoon and night off."

"You could have asked me," she said indignantly. How dare he take charge of her life just like that?

His eyes danced as he looked down at her. "I *am* asking you," he said.

"I won't go," she retorted.

"Fine. We're leaving at nine in the morning. We've got a lot of traveling ahead of us."

"Blake!"

"Eat your breakfast," he said with a wink. "You're going to need your strength."

And he strode off into the house, leaving her furious and frustrated.

chapter

6

"MR. KINCADE, I don't know if I'm right for this job anymore," Brittany said, walking into his den that afternoon.

Ambroise looked up from his afternoon chess game. Etienne, as always, discreetly said nothing. Sometimes, Brittany noted, it was hard even to realize he was there.

"Nonsense. I hired you, didn't I?" Ambroise said irritably.

"You also hired a lot of other people whom you let go," she reminded him, sitting down in a hard-backed chair next to the chess table.

"They never got as far as you have. You're doing a great job—and I don't give out praise liberally. I don't do anything liberally," he added under his breath. "Now you're staying and seeing this thing through, Britt. The clothes won't fit anyone else. End of discussion." He awarded her another dark scowl and went back to the game.

Brittany stayed stubbornly where she was.

"Well, what is it? Is it Blake?" Ambroise asked suddenly, looking up again, obviously annoyed.

"Yes. He keeps interrupting my work and I find that . . . it's difficult to concentrate at times."

Did she imagine the half-smile on Ambroise's lips?

"Look, Britt," he said, "I don't want you overworking either. Now maybe you can straighten Blake out, maybe you can't, but I'd rather see him with you than with those empty-headed little numbers he parades through here— if he bothers to bring them here at all. Mostly he brings them to our suite at the Biltmore."

Brittany's heart skipped a beat and a guilty blush covered her cheeks. That was where he had brought her. So another tryst was what he had had in mind all along. Well, she'd show him she wasn't just another "empty-headed little number."

". . . so stick it through," Ambroise was saying. "Get my great-grandmother's life in order and maybe, just maybe, you can help out my son. In the meantime, enjoy yourself. A lot of women would welcome the chance to be in your shoes."

"I'm sure a lot of women *have* been in my shoes," she said and marched out of the room.

"Great spunk, that girl," she heard Ambroise say, sounding pleased.

She looked back. Etienne silently moved his knight.

"Your great-great-grandson is persistent," Brittany said to the woman in the picture on her desk. Elizabeth's expression remained stoic. "I guess he gets that from you." Well, Elizabeth had lived through Indian raids and God only knew what else. Brittany supposed she herself could live through this. But why did he have to be so good-looking? And why did her blood rush every time he touched her? Why did she count the minutes until he might kiss her again? Why did she feel like a woman in a storybook, when he had no intention of "living happily after?"

Work, Brittany, work, she ordered herself, deliberately emptying her mind of everything but the papers in her hand. Elizabeth's story was coming along quite well. She had learned a lot from Elizabeth about the daily life

of the Apache, although Elizabeth did not provide a great
deal of detail. She wasn't interested in the Apache people
per se, but after her capture she learned that her very
survival would depend in part on how well she pleased
her captors. Her learning their ways pleased them greatly,
and made them more inclined to treat Elizabeth with
respect and kindness. As a result, she learned fast.

Brittany was surprised to discover that the Apaches
loved to tell stories about the adventures of brave warriors. Not unlike white men telling war stories, she
thought. The hardships, the rituals, the superstitions—
was the Apache way of life so very unlike the lives of
the early American settlers? No, Brittany decided, the
two groups shared very similar ways of life, and their
conflicts hardly differed from similar conflicts between
groups of peoole fought down through the centuries all
over the world. Man's pride ensured that he would fight
to win and maintain dominance over competing groups.
A people's language might be different, or its skin a
different hue, but the pride that beat within the human
breast was the same the world over.

Brittany noted down her thoughts as she read. Finally
she paused to rest and stretch. She was tired, more tired
than she had thought. But her fatigue wasn't just from
work. She was anticipating tomorrow, the long ride alone
with Blake. Which car would they take? One of the little
ones where their thighs touched, sending warm streams
of lightning through her? Was this the way it would
always be? Waiting for a chance to be with him, then
afraid when the chance came?

Wearily she closed the pages of Elizabeth's journal
and went outside for a walk.

The next day Brittany had still come to no conclusions
about how to resolve her dilemma with Blake. She was
too tired to think about it anymore. She was going to be

with him and that was all that mattered right now. There would be people at the party and on the way home he would probably be too tired to try to make love to her. She should be fairly safe. Standing in the driveway waiting for him, she smiled with genuine happiness as he came toward her from the house.

"All ready?" he asked amiably, taking her small carryall and putting it in the trunk. He had told her to wear something comfortable for the trip, that she could change once they arrived. She had chosen a turquoise sundress. She could tell by the way Blake looked at her that he approved of her choice.

"What's that?" he asked, pointing to the briefcase in her hand.

"Your great-great-grandmother. I thought I'd do some work while you drive."

"Good lord, you're an eager beaver." He shook his head.

"I wouldn't throw rocks if I were you," she said good-naturedly.

"No, I guess you're right. After all, you seem to be doing better with your project than I am with mine." His eyes shone with a devilish glint.

"Haven't you got something better to do than try to seduce me?" she asked as they roared away in the car.

"Nothing," he told her with a wink.

She sighed with exasperation and, avoiding his eyes, opened her briefcase.

A couple of hours later they stopped to eat lunch at an unpretentious diner along the main road. Several semi-trailer trucks parked outside made Brittany decide the restaurant must serve as a regular truck stop.

"No headwaiter to sneak us in," she commented as Blake helped her out of his low-slung sports car.

"Somehow I think we'll get a table," he told her, taking her arm as they walked in. The place was small and simple, but clean. "And I never sneak," he added. "When you're a self-confident person you walk in plain sight with your head held high."

"There's nothing *plain* about you," she murmured, playing on his words. She hadn't really meant for him to hear, but he picked up on the comment right away.

"Thanks. And I can heartily return the compliment now that you've stopped hiding behind that old school-marm hairdo."

Lately she *had* been wearing her hair down, she admitted to herself, but she hoped he didn't think she'd done so for his benefit. "I just wore my hair up to keep it out of the way—and I wasn't hiding," she protested.

"That's alright, because I found you out anyway," he told her playfully, covering her hand with his as they sat down at the counter. A truck driver two seats away moved in closer, sitting down right next to Brittany.

The waitress smiled appreciatively at Blake. "What'll you have?" she asked in a sultry voice.

"Two hamburgers and two coffees," Blake told her.

"I want a cheeseburger," Brittany corrected.

"You heard the lady," he said to the waitress, who didn't seem to be aware that someone else was present. Her rubber soles squeeked along the wooden floor as she shuffled off for the coffee. An unseen person in the back took care of the rest of the order.

"Ain't seen you around here before," muttered the bull of a man sitting at Brittany's elbow. "I come here often myself on my route to Flagstaff."

Blake glanced over at the man, clearly annoyed. "C'mon, Sacajawea," he said, "let's get a table." He took her hand and stood up.

"Hey, wait a minute," interrupted the trucker. "Maybe the lady don't want to take a table just yet. Maybe she wants to talk to a real man."

Suddenly Brittany found herself being tugged in opposite directions like a turkey wishbone. Blake had hold of one hand while the trucker gripped her other arm like a vice.

"Let me go," she said angrily to the trucker. "I don't know you and I have no intention of knowing you."

The waitress turned from the coffee urn, looking distressed. "Jake, sit down. I don't want any trouble here."

"No trouble, Belle. I was just starting a nice conversation with the lady here when hotshot tries to bust it up." In a series of lightning-fast movements he shoved Blake back with one hamlike hand. Blake stumbled, caught his balance, and came forward with flying fists. A right cross to the man's chin and a left to his stomach sent him sprawling on the floor with a loud thud. He sat slowly, shaking his head, stunned.

Blake took Brittany's hand and headed for the door. "Come on, let's get out of here. Suddenly I don't like the atmosphere. Cancel the cheeseburger," he added over his shoulder.

"Did he hurt you?" Brittany asked once they were back in the car. She studied Blake's hand with concern as they sped onto the highway with a spurt of gravel.

"No, but I wasn't about to stay and let him get another crack at it. He was built like a brick wall. My knuckles still ache from connecting with his jaw."

They looked red and swollen from what Brittany could see. "I'm sorry you had to go through that for me," she apologized.

"That's okay," he said, dismissing the incident. Then he stopped. "Hey, don't Indians have a custom whereby if you save their life it becomes yours to do with as you please?"

"No, you've got that confused with the Chinese," Brittany corrected. But she knew what was coming.

"Okay," he agreed. "Does that mean your virtue is now mine?"

"Only if I'm Chinese," she told him.

"Your eyes are almond-shaped." He smiled at her wickedly.

She laughed. "Blake, don't you ever give up?" she cried, amused in spite of herself.

Their eyes met warmly. "I play to win, remember?" he said huskily.

For once she had no answer.

They arrived at the party hungry, not having wanted to take any more time to stop and eat. Brittany felt she'd grown closer to Blake—as was natural, she decided, considering what they had just shared. However old-fashioned it sounded, Blake was her "protector," and she felt a special glow when she looked at him.

The house in which the party was being held was a Spanish hacienda that reminded Brittany of the type belonging to cattle barons in old movies. It struck her as being bigger than life, although it wasn't as large as Ambroise's. An attractive woman with a bright smile came out to greet them, and Brittany immediately felt at ease. Molly Anderson didn't stand on formality.

Blake had told Brittany that Molly had come to wealth through hard work and had never lost the qualities of simple warmth and sincerity that had endeared her to her late husband. The second time around she had been able to afford to marry a younger man. Johnny Anderson was twelve years her junior, but could hardly keep up with her in spirit. She had more energy at forty-two than most women had at twenty-one.

"Hello, Blake," Molly said, giving him a hug which expressed genuine affection rather than the kind of showy but artificial joviality Brittany had often seen exhibited among high-society people. "A lot of others are already here." Molly cast smiling eyes at Brittany. "And who's this?"

"This is a waif I picked up along the way," Blake said.

"I work for Blake's father," Brittany told the woman with a warm smile. "My name is Brittany Sinclair."

"Well, welcome, Brittany. My house is your house. Anything you want, just ask," Molly said grandly, gesturing toward the well-lit structure.

"I really would like to freshen up," Brittany said, her body aching from being cramped in the sports car.

"Of course, of course, let me take you to your room." Molly put a friendly arm around Brittany's shoulders and, with Blake on the other side, led them into the house.

"You're taking me to my room?" Brittany asked, surprised.

"Well, of course. Didn't you know? You're spending the night. I wouldn't have Blake driving back in the condition he's bound to be in by the time the party's over," Molly explained, laughing.

Over Molly's head Blake smiled mischievously at Brittany, who turned her face away, annoyed. Why hadn't he told her he intended to stay overnight? He had no right just to assume she'd go along with his plans—or to trick her into a compromising situation like this one.

Molly led them down a cool hallway to a large room done all in white and situated so that it did not get the afternoon sun. After she and Blake left, Brittany changed quickly, slipping out of one dress and into another in record time, afraid that Blake would throw open the door at any moment. She wouldn't put it past him. She was fiddling with the zipper when she heard a knock on the door.

"Blake?" she asked, angling for the elusive zipper.

"Sorry, it's only me, Molly," said her hostess. "May I come in?"

Brittany opened the door, still struggling.

"Here, let me," Molly offered, turning her around. Although perfectly coiffured and made up, looking not unlike a model in a high-fashion magazine, Molly had a motherly quality about her. "Blake's already outside so I thought I'd lead the way," she said kindly.

"He didn't wait?" Brittany asked. Of course, why should he? These were his friends and she was . . . what? His challenge, that was all. She regained her composure and hid her disappointment. "That's very nice of you, Mrs. Anderson."

"I'm Molly to my friends," the woman said easily. "We are going to be friends, aren't we?"

"Well, yes, of course. But my position in Blake's house is only temporary. I'm working on a project for his father and—"

Molly interrupted with one wave of a bejeweled hand. "I wouldn't count on the temporary part. Ready?" she asked.

Brittany slipped on her high-heeled sandals and nodded. Her heart was beating fast. "What makes you say that?" she asked, following Molly out. "Did Blake say anything?" She wondered if she sounded as eager as she thought she did.

"No, but I've known Blake a long time. My late husband Sidney and I used to get together quite often with Blake's parents. I just have a sense, that's all. Oh, there's Johnny. Johnny!" She waved and called to her husband, a man of medium build with blond hair who was standing some distance away near the pool.

Hearing his name, he flashed a bright smile in their direction. Brittany found it hard to picture Molly married to him, but Johnny seemed quite happy as he walked over to join them.

"Brittany, this is my husband. Johnny, this is Blake's new flame."

Johnny reached out and pumped Brittany's hand.

"Boy, are there going to be a lot of women here who'd like to scratch your eyes out," he exclaimed with teasing lightness.

Brittany didn't know whether to correct the piece of misinformation about being Blake's new flame, or to just enjoy it. She chose the latter. The truth would be out soon enough, she speculated. It was nice to be thought of as Blake's girlfriend, even for the afternoon. She was sure the position had a high rate of turnover.

"Blake's showing better taste in his old age," Johnny added with a laugh. "Stick with him, Brittany. He's a rogue, but I've never known a better friend. He was the one who introduced me to Molly here. I'll always be grateful." Johnny's eyes grew tender as he gazed affectionately at the woman at his side. "C'mon, I'll show you around," he said, taking hold of Brittany's arm and leading her toward the pool. She scanned the area for Blake, but didn't see him.

"He's around here somewhere, mingling," Johnny assured her, his voice just a touch uneasy. He was steering her away from the partially screened gazebo that stood off to the left against a wall of leylandii cypresses.

"Have you known him a long time?" Brittany asked, wanting to know everything about Blake.

Johnny smiled. "Forever. We went to school together, shared our first drink together, you name it. He's always been an A-number one guy. When Molly's husband died, Blake stepped in to help her with the estate. He saved her from a lawyer who would have robbed her blind. He saved her for me, as it turned out. All I ever did for him was show him the finer points of racing. Since I met Molly, I've stopped racing altogether. Unfortunately, that was around the same time Blake started. He's damned good, but he takes too many chances, and I don't think his father will ever welcome me into the house because of it."

"Blake's racing frightens me," Brittany admitted, a

shiver passing over her as she thought of the danger involved, the tremendous risks he took each time he sat behind the wheel. "But it's not your fault," she told Johnny as they walked about the pool area.

"Thanks for the vote of confidence," he said. "But I do hold myself responsible."

"He's doing it because of his wife's death," she argued. "If not racing, there'd be something else."

"Are you a psychiatrist?" Johnny asked, apparently amused.

"Worse, a minister's daughter. We hold the hands of people who can't afford a psychiatrist—which was everyone in the town I came from."

"You really are a delight." Johnny laughed warmly. "If Molly didn't have me sewed up, and if Blake weren't my best friend, I'd be after you myself right now."

"Thank you. I think I needed that," Brittany said, glancing at the well-groomed, polished women who stood about in small groups, chatting and laughing. Brittany wondered if their hair ever got out of place or if their makeup ever looked other than perfect.

Johnny seemed to read her mind. "You're the best-looking one here. Barring Molly," he added loyally.

Brittany was about to respond when she heard a high-pitched laugh on her left. She turned to see Blake stepping out from the shade of the gazebo, Sheila on his arm.

"Eh, don't mind that," Johnny said, clearly trying to draw Brittany away. "Sheila can be all over the man she sets her sights on."

"Blake has two legs," Brittany said angrily. "He could walk away." Then, sensing Johnny's uneasiness, she immediately softened her tone. "That's alright, Johnny. There's nothing between us, really." Nothing but chemistry, she thought, and a desire that mounted all the time. "I'm working for his father, and when the job is finished I'll be leaving. He just needed some company for the day."

At that moment Brittany saw a woman whose dress seemed to be held up only at the defiance of gravity come up excitedly behind Blake and throw her arms around him.

"Blake, it's been forever!" she squealed, kissing him lustily on the cheek. She relaxed her grip on him but appeared ready to linger with her arms still loosely around him. But Sheila, uttering an oath, gave her a none-too-gentle shove that upset her balance. With a wild shriek and a loud splash, the woman toppled backwards into the pool. The crowd cried out as several onlookers were sprayed with water and people shifted away from the edge, where they talked with renewed animation.

Hurling angry expletives that brought amused expressions to people's faces, the drenched woman scrambled up the pool ladder and ran after Sheila, who was caught in the woman's strong grip before she had a chance to escape. Johnny raced over to separate the two furious women, all the while trying to make light of the situation to his guests.

"That's one way to cool off, Rhonda," he joked. "I don't allow my women guests to kiss men who are spoken for—unless, of course, it's me." Obviously taking Johnny to mean her rather than Brittany, Sheila turned a triumphant face toward Rhonda.

"See, everyone knows Blake and I are together, even though we didn't arrive that way," she said. "Oh Blake, darling, I missed you so. That's why I came back earlier than planned. I'll never take another vacation without you."

So that was it, Brittany thought. Sheila had been on vacation. That was why Blake had spent so much time with her, Brittany, taking her to the theater and to this party. Sheila hadn't been around.

Brittany turned away from Blake before he could see the disappointment in her face. Molly was rushing by with a towel for Rhonda, but she came to a full stop beside Brittany. "Are you alright?" she asked anxiously. "You look like you just lost your best friend."

Brittany shook her head. "There's something in the air, and I'm not feeling well. I think I'll go lie down for a bit."

"You'll do no such thing," Molly chided, taking hold of her arm. "You'll dance and eat and flirt and have a good time. Don't let Sheila turn you into a wallflower."

"No, really, I don't belong here," Brittany said, thinking to herself that she didn't know where she belonged anymore. Back home had been too confining, but this world was too heady, too full of hurt.

"Now, you listen to me," Molly said sternly, taking her aside, apparently forgetting the dripping woman at the pool. "There's no such thing as belonging and not belonging. You make your own place in this world. When I first met my late husband I didn't think I had a chance in the world, but he saw things in me that I didn't see in myself. And now I'm a mature woman who's got a younger husband. That didn't go down well either in the beginning, but now it does, because I make it work. Sheila is a gorgeous creature with the heart of a viper, and if Blake loses all the good sense he's always had and winds up with her, it'll be the end of him. Do you want that to happen?"

"No," Brittany said. It still didn't help the way she felt right then, and she was sure Molly saw much more in the situation than there was, no matter how much Brittany wished it were otherwise.

"Then do as I say and bring that man to his senses," Molly urged.

"Molly!" Johnny called. "Rhonda's drying out in the sun."

"Coming," she called cheerfully. "Now that the natives have had their entertainment, let's move on to the buffet tables," she urged the crowd in a loud voice. The guests laughed and did as she suggested, wandering slowly to the side tables filled with food.

"You come with me," she ordered Brittany.

Blake was being dragged off by Sheila, who looked dazzling in an off-the-shoulder blue dress. The plunging neckline stopped practically at her navel, leaving little to the imagination. She pressed her breast against Blake's arm as they headed toward the buffet table.

Blake was trying to catch Brittany's eye, but she pretended not to see him. What did he want—three women fighting over him? She stayed with Molly, who after taking care of Rhonda promptly went about with Brittany, introducing her to every available bachelor at the party. Brittany's head swam with names and faces, very few of which matched. She made an honest effort, though, to study the people who populated Blake's world and tried to get into the spirit of the party. She found that, with very little effort, she was having fun meeting new people. But, all the while, despite the attentions of several attractive men, her thoughts kept returning to Blake.

The evening wore on and, as pleasant music filtered through the air, Brittany found herself dancing with first one man and then another.

"Do I need a ticket?" Blake asked, cutting in on one of his friends.

"Where's your leash? Did Sheila set you free?" Brittany asked coldly.

"Look, I'm sorry about Sheila. I didn't know she was going to be here."

"Obviously," Brittany said sarcastically. "Why else would you have invited me?"

"I invited you because I wanted your company," he told her, pulling her closer to him. "Because you're so easy to talk to and nice to be around. No accusations."

"No promises," she said under her breath.

"I don't offer empty words, if that's what you mean by that," he told her. "Would you like me to plight my troth?" His expression was half amused, half annoyed.

"You wouldn't mean it anyway," she scoffed.

"And if I did?" he challenged, his face lowering toward hers and nuzzling her gently. "You smell good," he murmured.

Why was he doing this to her? Did he want her to bare her soul, tell him she loved him, and then be left standing with empty dreams while he laughed over it with Sheila or Rhonda or a dozen others.

But before she could confront him with her questions, a chiding voice called out, "There you are, entertaining the employees again," and Sheila came up behind them. "Honestly, Blake," she added, "sometimes your sense of fair play goes too far. This is our dance, darling." Her voice had a nasty edge to it. Blake appeared ready to answer Sheila sharply, but Brittany stepped away from him first.

"Yes, master, thank you for your kindness," she said coldly. "I wouldn't dare stand in the way of two people who deserve each other so much."

She was immediately sorry for her childish retort, but nevertheless she walked quickly away, heading for her room and solitude. Why had she said that? Blake had said he enjoyed her company. Other times he'd hinted that he found her refreshingly different from the other women he knew. But that was just it. He saw her as a brief pause in his life, a commercial before he returned to the main program—to Sheila and all the others. He belonged with that viper Sheila—and she herself belonged...she belonged in Blake's arms, Brittany thought miserably.

Hurriedly she went down the hall to her room and shut the door. After changing out of her dress into the fresh, lacy nightgown Molly had had laid out for her, Brittany sat down and opened her briefcase. There was no use sitting about feeling sorry for herself. She might as well be productive. Reading about Elizabeth would take her mind off Blake.

Brittany tried to shut out the laughter and music from the party as she started reading. She willed her mind to fade away from today and go back to the past, before there were artificial people who didn't really care about their supposed friends and "modern" values that seemed just plain wrong to her. She began to read about Elizabeth.

The only time I thought of killing myself was when I learned I was with child. A child of neither world. A half-breed. Could my heart stand it? Happily I did not offend God by taking the life of my child and myself. The child, my son, was my greatest comfort and joy in the five years of my captivity. There came a time when I gave up hope, gave up waiting for the rescue party that never came. And soon, as my place became apparent, as I was grudgingly accepted by the women of the tribe, and thus by their daughters and sons, I ceased to want the rescue party to arrive. There came a day when I actually feared they would come and intrude upon the world that was now mine.

I grew to love my husband, for that was the way I came to look upon him, married to him alone in my heart even though he kept his other wives. He shared his triumphs and his silences with me. I could tell that I pleased him by learning the ways of his people and by trying hard to form the words that were familiar to him. I know he loved me too.

Brittany set down the pages, once more impressed with the character of the woman she was reading about. She jotted down some notes so that she'd be able to relate the story to Ambroise the next day.

As she was putting her work away, a knock sounded on her door. Probably Molly, coming to see about her. But when she opened the door, Blake strode into the room and closed the door behind him, not waiting for her to invite him in.

"I've come to claim what's mine," he said abruptly. Caught off guard, she looked at him, puzzled. "I saved your virtue this afternoon, remember?"

"You don't honestly mean..."

The grin on his face grew wider, his engaging smile tugging at her heart, as it always did. Hang on, Brittany, she commanded herself as his eyes began to pull her toward him, calling to something within her. Suddenly the image of Sheila laughing on Blake's arm came to her and her desire turned to anger.

"Get out," she ordered calmly, pointing to the door.

"I promise you'll enjoy it," he persisted, taking hold of her hand. She pulled it away.

"I'm sure you've had a lot of practice perfecting your technique, but I'm not interested," she told him.

"I think you are interested," he replied, taking hold of her again. "I want you, Brittany. I want you very badly." His voice was soft, the words caressing her face like hot fleeting kisses.

"What's the matter? Everyone else turn you down?" she asked sarcastically, beginning to melt inside, fighting for control. "Or have you gone through them all by now?"

"You're talking like a fool," he warned her.

"I know I'm a fool, but it's for a different reason."

"I don't want to spend the rest of tonight talking," he told her, then pulled her into his arms so suddenly that she gasped. The papers in her hand slipped from her fingers and scattered about the floor like dry leaves before a storm.

Blake's hot mouth drew her breath into him as he kissed her hard and long, melting her resistence in a fire she had come to know so well. Time and the world stood still beneath the onslaught of his lips. She could barely think. Something in her resisted the thoughts that struggled to the surface. The indignation she had felt this afternoon was a million miles away, as was everything else but the growing ache within her.

His hands caressed the curves of her body, touching her possessively, intimately. He kissed her mouth, his tongue sliding hot and moist over hers, until she was limp in his arms. And still he pressed her against him.

"See how well we fit together?" he murmured, pushing her backward until her legs were trapped by the edge of the bed. The teasing note in his voice brought her up short. Something was wrong, very wrong. It just wouldn't mean the same thing to him as it would to her. If she gave in to him, let him make love to her, she would feel wedded to him, body and soul, forever. But to him she would be just one of many, the last in a long string of conquests.

"No!" she said so loudly that she thought the whole house heard. But it was really no more than a hoarse whisper in her throat.

"Who are you saying that to, you or me?" Blake asked, pausing but not releasing her. "I can see into your soul, Sacajawea, better than you can."

"Leave me alone," she pleaded. "If you had a shred of decency in you, you'd leave me alone." She couldn't take this torture much longer. If he pressed his suit, she would give in, despite all her resolutions and good sense.

"But you already said I don't have a shred of decency, remember? I'm the rogue who leaves a trail of women behind him," he teased, but his eyes were serious. "Don't be afraid," he implored. He kissed her neck. "I'll be gentle."

His voice was thick with a desire she yearned to satisfy. But she pulled away from him, forcing herself to relinquish his warm and tender touch. "I'm not afraid," she said calmly, carefully, slowly regaining her control.

"I just don't want to be one of the women in your life. I'm not like your great-great-grandmother."

"What's that got to do with it?" he demanded.

"I won't settle for being one of the squaws. She had no choice. I do! Now go back to Sheila before she comes looking for you again. I wouldn't want to be part of a scandal."

His sudden anger was like an electric current flashing between them. "Your trouble is you don't want to be part of anything except the past, Brittany," he accused her hotly, heading for the door. "The past is nice and safe for you. You peek into other people's lives and see how they lived rather than living yourself. Well, since you keep urging me to go back to Sheila, I will. At least every conversation I have with her doesn't end up with recriminations tossed in my face."

"I don't care where you go," she cried out, turning her back on him and clenching her fists at her sides.

But even as he slammed the door behind him she knew she did care.

chapter

7

AT BREAKFAST THE next morning Blake looked like he hadn't slept all night. He said very little to Brittany. Pressing her lips together bitterly, she wondered if Sheila had kept him up. Yet even as her heart twisted with pain, she realized it had been her own fault. She had sent Blake straight into Sheila's arms. Sheila had received the kisses and embraces meant for her.

Blake remained silent on the long ride home. At first Brittany felt at ease just sitting next to him, but gradually the silence began to bother her. She had never been on bad terms with anyone, and she kept hoping Blake would say something to break the ice, but time passed by and he remained shut up with his own thoughts. Growing increasingly restless and uncomfortable, Brittany found it hard to concentrate on her work.

"Why aren't you reading?" Blake asked suddenly, his voice casual.

"I . . . I can't seem to concentrate," she stammered.

"Guilt will do that to you," he said with a knowing lilt in his voice.

"Guilt?" She half turned in her seat. "What do I have to be guilty about?"

"Sending me off into the cold like that, when there was nothing in my heart but pure fire for you."

"You wouldn't know 'pure' if it bit you," she retorted, feeling relieved now that Blake had reestablished communication and redrawn the lines of battle.

"Sure I'd know 'pure,'" he told her, stopping at a red light as they entered the center of Phoenix. He reached out to touch her hair. "It very nearly did bite me last night."

"If you'd only behave, I wouldn't have yelled like that," she explained, half apologizing.

"If I behaved, this would be a dull relationship. Now I'd like to call a truce to this warring encounter of ours—which doesn't mean you're to feel safe from me," he added naughtily. Part of her was immediately glad. Why? she asked herself. Was she crazy? Was love always total madness? "It's just that I have to go on a trip for a few days and I hate leaving problems behind," Blake was saying.

"You're leaving?" she echoed.

He put his hand over hers. "Unless you'd like to come with me. There's a race in central California."

"A race? I thought the doctor told you—"

"Words that my dad put into his mouth," he interrupted. "I can't skip this race. It would put me out of the running for the championship."

"And it will put you into the running for a grave," Brittany snapped, thoroughly annoyed.

"Hey, no more hot words, okay?" Blake asked as they drove on. His hand tightened on hers.

She shrugged, angry but helpless to do anything about it. Her words meant nothing to him. If he really cared about her, he wouldn't be doing this, tempting fate as if he wanted to join his wife in death. For the first time Brittany's heart was filled with jealousy for the woman Blake had loved—and lost. Immediately she chastised herself for such sinful thoughts.

"It's your funeral," she said lightly, trying to act as

if she didn't care. She turned away to hide her real feelings.

"Maybe I'll disappoint you and live," Blake answered.

"It won't be me you'll be disappointing."

"No psychology now, Sacajawea." Blake pulled the sports car into the Kincade driveway and turned to look down at her fondly. "Ah, if I had more time I'd whisk you into my room and show you how I'll never disappoint you." Then, to Brittany's surprise, he pulled her roughly into his arms, his hands like steel bands on her, and kissed her long and hard. He leaped out of the car. "I've got a lot of packing to do," he called back as he ran up the stairs, leaving her sitting there alone.

Half an hour later Brittany went in search of Blake. She found him in his room, just shutting his suitcase.

"To what do I owe this visit?" he asked as she entered.

"Be careful," she said softly, her eyes serious. "Just— be careful. I'm afraid every time you take hold of the wheel."

She could see that she had touched him with her concern, and he put his arm around her. "Don't worry. No matter what you think, I've still got a few things left to do before my number's up. I want to win, not die." He ran his finger along her mouth, tracing the soft fullness of her lips. "Will this be waiting for me when I get back?" he asked.

"I haven't finished with the book," she told him, evading his real question, finding it difficult to meet his eyes.

The smile that covered his face was amused, although just a bit sad. "I'm not the only one who fails to make certain commitments," he told her and then he kissed her swiftly. "Wish I could stay, but there are people waiting." He touched the tip of her nose in a tender gesture. "See you, Sacajawea."

He walked out, and she stood where she was, as still as a statue. Then she ran down the stairs after him, wanting to see him out the door.

But from the top of the stairs she saw Sheila standing there, looking beautiful in a sundress that was practically frontless.

"Hi, honey. I wore silver to match the car," she told Blake, kissing him hello.

"What are you doing here?" he asked in a tone of surprise—or could it be anger? Brittany wondered.

"Why, I'm going with you to be your good luck charm, just like always," she said. "Some of the others are driving along too. Do hurry, darling." She led the way outside, provocatively swaying her hips. Blake's response was muffled as the door closed behind them.

A stab of jealousy shot through Brittany and she ran down the stairs, seeking refuge in the library and Elizabeth's journals.

Brittany missed Blake terribly, despite her anger and jealousy and her overall confusion. Her jealousy irritated her in particular. She knew what Blake was—a playboy. And he was very good at it. Naturally he was charming to her. A man didn't seduce a woman by being brutal, and seduction was certainly his goal. He'd been honest about that much at least. Why did she keep trying to make more of their relationship? Why did she persist in holding onto the sweet memories of his lips on hers, the urgent pressure of his body against hers? Romance wasn't supposed to be like this, a heady wine. It was supposed to be calm and strong and reassuring, the way life had been with Jonathan. But life with Jonathan had never had the thrill that life with Blake held for her now.

Ambroise commented on Brittany's change in mood one day after lunch. "You seem to be rather withdrawn these days," he said. "Isn't the book going well?"

"Oh yes, it's going very well," she hastened to assure him. "I'm just lagging behind a little . . ."

"No need to hurry with it. I'm afraid I've put a little too much pressure on you about it. I mean I know Elizabaeth's story in general. It's just that I was, and am, hungry for her own words. It's like having my own link to the past, I guess." He took out his pipe and tobacco pouch, then almost furtively looked over his shoulder. "My doctor and Etienne don't approve of my smoking," he confided to Brittany, "and Etienne can be almost a persimmon about matters. No wonder he never stayed with any of his wives." He began drawing on his pipe, trying to get it lit. "Your sparkle's down," he commented bluntly. "Is it Blake?"

Caught unprepared, Brittany shrugged, not knowing what to answer.

"The boy and I really don't get along, at least not in words," Ambroise went on. "But he's got good qualities under all that, Britt. Qualities of kindness and caring. Anne's death left him hollow."

"He seems to have enough women to fill up any hollow," Brittany commented, and Ambroise laughed.

"He's a good-looking man, like I was once, before I became a leathery old one."

"You're not old," Brittany contradicted with a fond smile. Ambroise had been like a father to her since she'd arrived at the house. Like a warm, supportive father.

"Good, jump in on the right parts, Britt. Disagree with me. I like that." They smiled at one another. "That hollow has to be filled by the right woman, and it will be eventually, after Blake plays out his hurt—provided the mortuary doesn't get him first. I'll be glad when he stops racing," he added with a sigh. Then he looked up at her. "Well, get to it, Britt. Tell me my story for today," he commanded. "What have you got?"

Brittany picked up her notes and began to read, aware

that Ambroise was watching her intently. Was he beginning to think of her as a match for his son? If only Blake
saw her in that light. But playboys didn't make commitments like marriage, especially if they had been
burned once, the way Blake had. His father's wishes
would have no bearing on the matter, she concluded
sadly.

Later, after Ambroise had left, her head ached from
all the close reading she had done that day, for Elizabeth's
handwriting was cramped at best. Brittany called it a day
earlier than usual and went out by the pool to relax. With
Blake gone there was no one in the house except the
servants and Ambroise, so she had the pool all to herself.
There were none of Blake's friends to come over and
make her feel like an outsider. That was what she was,
she thought, rubbing suntan lotion on her body and remembering the feel of Blake's strong fingers as he had
done it for her that day on the lake. No matter what she
thought, she was an outsider. But as good as any of
them, she told herself proudly, tossing her ash-blond hair
behind her shoulders. But she belonged in another world,
not their world—or did she? She thought back to what
she had read that afternoon.

The rescue party has come. Cochise has agreed to
go back to the reservation, allowing the white men
to make good their word in another treaty. But I
am to go back to my people. My people. Who are
my people now? I do not think I belong to either
world any longer, for I am white, but long to follow
my husband, who is not. He is better off with his
squaws, who can give him full-blooded Apaches,
and I am better off—where? I will be the object
of pity or scorn among the whites for allowing an
Indian to father my son. If only I could go away
somewhere by myself. I wish it had never hap-

pened, but then I would never have known Nachise, and for all that I would be sad. He is a man
like no other and I shall always love him and the
son he gave to me. But the treaty insists on pris-
oners being returned and in white eyes I am a
prisoner. Little do they realize that I long ago chose
to stay. What is to become of me?

And what was to become of she herself, Brittany
wondered, bringing the question into the present. She
could not stay in the Kincade house forever. Eventually
she would finish the book, and she would never prolong
work on it just to satisfy her own end. That would be
unfair to Mr. Kincade. Besides, the longer she stayed,
the harder it would be to leave. She sighed and began
to rise in the chair to go inside.

But a shadow fell over her. She looked up to see Blake
standing there. He had come home and found her! He
was always finding her, she thought. Her happiness at
seeing him was instantaneous as he took her without
ceremony into his arms. Then she remembered that the
last time she had seen him Sheila had been with him.
She grew unresponsive to his touch.

"Well, that kiss certainly tapered off," Blake said
dryly, letting her go. "That's no way to treat the con-
quering hero."

"Where's Sheila?" she asked coldly.

"Where she belongs. Listen, Sheila invited herself
along on the trip. It's a free country. I couldn't very well
tell her not to come."

"Of course not," Brittany agreed sarcastically.

"Don't start up again, Sacajawea." He sounded angry.
"It's too nice a day for that. I've come to change and to
rescue you."

"I don't need any rescuing," she told him firmly.

"Yes, you do." He traced the faint lines under her

eyes. "That shows you've been working late into the night. Obviously in an attempt to keep your mind off me."

"Why you big, insufferable, conceited—"

He pulled her close to him. "Them's fighting words, lady," he whispered huskily. "But I never hit a lady. I believe in some nonbrotherly love." With that he kissed her again. This time it was no fleeting greeting, but a reacquaintance with the passion that lay beneath the protests and the wall she tried to erect around her. She tried to push against his chest to ward him off, but he caught her hands and brought them down to her sides. Soon she wasn't struggling anymore. His lips were moving persuasively against hers, taking her breath away, melting her lingering resistance.

"There, that's better," he told her, his voice not as mocking as it had been before. "Now get ready. I have a picnic in mind for us. Be ready in half an hour—unless, of course, you'd rather go dressed like that," he added, his eyes sweeping over the white bathing suit she wore, noting the way it hugged her curves and accentuated her small waist and sensuous hips. She felt almost nude before him.

"I'll put something on," she said hastily and ran into the house in her bare feet.

"Drat," she heard him say behind her and, despite her determination not to be swayed by him, she found herself smiling.

When she met Blake in front of the house thirty minutes later, dressed in blue jeans and a cotton shirt, she was surprised to find he had two horses saddled and waiting, with what looked like a large picnic basket slung over the saddle horn of his own horse.

She couldn't help breaking into a wide grin. "What are you smiling about?" he asked, smiling back at her.

"I just never pictured you on a horse."

"There are a lot of things you don't know about me,

Sacajawea," he told her, only half joking. "The horses are mine. We usually board them at the track, but since I know you can ride I thought you might enjoy something different this time around."

"Is that a promise? Can we just talk and be friends for the afternoon?" she asked, putting her foot into the stirrup and swinging up into the saddle.

Blake watched her fluid motion with appreciation. "Boy scout's honor," he said.

"You've sworn that to me before," she reminded him, throwing him a suspicious look.

"Oh, yeah," was all he said. "C'mon, I thought you'd enjoy riding by Camelback Mountain. The country's really pretty around there. It hardly even looks like Arizona."

He wasn't wrong. It was a perfect day for riding. The sky was crystal blue and the mountains reached up as if to touch it. Tall pines covered the hillsides. The summer breeze teased Brittany's hair and whipped it playfully about her face as they cantered to a spot Blake had already picked out for them.

He led Brittany to a secluded area just past an old cottage that looked like it hadn't been used for years. A weathered old tree offered a little shade as they looked down on a beautiful view of the valley.

Blake stepped over to help Brittany off her horse. He took hold of her waist and slid her off her horse, bringing their bodies in close enough contact to make warm color come to her cheeks.

"Behave," she warned him sternly once he'd set her on her feet, "or I'll make my getaway."

"You would, too, wouldn't you?" Blake laughed as he lifted the basket off the saddle horn. Brittany took it from him and began to arrange the blanket, a task which required two to smooth it out, for the breeze had picked up and insisted on ruffling it each time she tried to anchor it down.

"Now then, what's in here?" she asked, lifting the lid.

"I don't know. I just told Etienne to have the cook prepare an average feast, nothing fancy, you know." He winked. "The only thing I did ask for was wine—and two glasses. Although just having you here is heady enough for me."

Brittany looked over at him as he reclined on one elbow, his eyes studying her lazily. "You've got enough blarney in you for any three people I know," she accused him, embarrassed by his scrutiny.

"Blarney. Does that mean you're Irish?" he asked.

"A little," she admitted, taking cold fried chicken and paper plates out of the basket.

Blake picked a white flower from a saguaro cactus and tucked it behind her ear. Surprised by the gesture, she felt as if she had been kissed ever so softly.

"Who are you, Indian maiden?" Blake asked softly.

"I'm not the one with Indian blood," she countered. "You are."

He put his hand to his breast in a dramatic gesture. "You mean great-great-grandmother was indiscreet?"

"Great-great-grandmother didn't have a choice," Brittany told him.

"I kind of like that," Blake said, eyeing her form.

Although she felt on fire from his gaze, Brittany continued as if he hadn't said a word. She pushed a napkin toward him. "She was lucky that Cochise's son singled her out."

"Cochise?" Blake asked, sounding interested.

"Yes. Didn't you know? You've got some of his blood in you. From Elizabeth's journals and what I've read elsewhere, he seems to have been a kind and noble man."

"Who killed people," Blake added, obviously baiting her.

"They lied to him, took his land, and killed his brother

and nephews at a peace conference. Wouldn't you get angry?" Brittany challenged him.

A dark look came into his eyes, and she could almost see the Indian in him. "Yes, I would," he said quietly.

They ate in silence for a few moments, Brittany wondering what was going on in Blake's mind. Then she asked, "How did you know I could ride a horse? I never told you."

"You haven't told me a lot of things," he said. "I asked Etienne. He seems to know everything. He's the kind of nonentity that everyone is always saying things to, like a father confessor."

"I like him. I like your father too," she said, nibbling on a chicken thigh.

"What about me?" Blake asked, sitting up and moving closer.

She took a deep breath and paused, then said, "Of course I like you. I wouldn't be here if I didn't."

"Tell me more," he urged, his blue eyes shimmering.

She put down the chicken thigh she was holding. "Where I come from, women don't say things like this. Besides, you know I like your company," she said, feeling comfortable. "You're an interesting person. Now eat your chicken."

"There's far too much food here," Blake said, apparently willing to let her off the hook. Brittany felt relieved. "And I ate a big meal before I came."

"Then why a picnic?" she asked, a new nervousness beating inside her. She shouldn't have allowed herself to come with him. Already her pulse was beginning to quicken.

"So I could show you another side to me—the country boy who likes down-to-earth activities like riding horses in the country and eating Southern fried chicken. I'm not an ogre."

"I never thought you were. You just take advantage,

that's all," Brittany said as he drew still nearer to her. She felt herself weakening as the old yearning grew stronger within her.

"Any chance I get," Blake agreed in a voice barely above a whisper. He reached out and touched her hair. She'd hidden it under a bright green scarf, but he pulled the scarf free and her hair fell about her shoulders like a dark golden cloud.

"I like it better that way," he told her, his hand going down to the back of her neck, massaging it slowly, causing all her nerve endings to weaken and tensely wait for more.

As she arched her neck under his touch, she noticed that, above them, dark clouds were beginning to gather, threatening to break through the stickiness that had overtaken the land. Neither of them had noticed it earlier, each apparently wrapped up in the other. The coming storm reminded Brittany of the battle within her heart.

"You said you'd be good," she protested as he continued to caress her hair, neck, and back, his strong fingers working like magic on her taut nerves. Her protest became more faint.

"I will be good," Blake promised huskily as he took her into his arms and kissed her waiting lips.

His long, hungry kiss dissolved into a myriad of smaller ones. He kissed the corners of her mouth, her eyes, her nose. He nibbled gently on her earlobes and breathed softly into her ears, sending tingles down to her toes. She felt as if she were covered in a blanket of desire that left her aching for more, aching for him. He pulled her closer and then lowered her to the blanket, never stopping his kisses, never letting her recover her control.

Brittany had meant to push him back, but her arms had turned against her, and she pulled him even closer, her fingertips entwining in his jet-black hair. She felt his fingers undoing the buttons of her blouse, but no words came to her lips to stop him. His lips were on hers, drinking her in, pulling her away from herself, her rules, her very being. She was being engulfed by him.

A crack of thunder broke into the timeless world that was opening up about them. Heavy drops of rain fell onto the dry land, turning quickly into angry waves of water that came down in sheets.

They were drenched within moments. Blake jumped to his feet to grab the whinnying horses, leaving Brittany dazed and breathless, the feel of his body still filling her senses. Another crack of thunder rang out, louder than the first, and the horses pulled free from Blake's grasp and galloped away from him.

"Quick, we can make a run for the garden house!" he shouted to Brittany.

They headed for the small cottage they had passed earlier but were soaked to the skin by the time they reached its shelter. Blake thrust open the unlocked door and they hurried inside, then stood trying to catch their breath.

Brittany looked about the dusty room. The only furniture was a table and two chairs, a tiny combination refrigerator-stove-sink off in a corner, and a bed with a brass headboard. Rusty tools littered the sides. The cottage looked as if it had belonged to a caretaker, Brittany decided. The light switch refused to work, the power apparently long since shut off. Blake rummaged about and found candles of various sizes and a box of old matches.

"It's going to be dark soon," Brittany said, shivering in her wet clothes. "I'm sorry about the horses."

Blake nodded. "Couldn't be helped. I'll send someone from the stable to find them tomorrow. They'll be alright." Brittany sneezed. "But I don't know if I can say the same about you."

She shook her head. "It's just so dusty in here. This doesn't look like it's been used in years."

"It hasn't. You'd better get out of those wet clothes."

"And into what, pray tell?"

"How about my waiting arms?" he offered, grinning.

"No, thank you." She pushed her wet hair out of her face. She wished it weren't getting so dark.

"You'll catch pneumonia if you stay in those clothes."

"I'll catch something else if I don't," she told him, walking away to stand by the window.

"You're afraid of me, aren't you?" Blake said, coming up behind her.

She turned to face him. He wasn't more than an inch away and the smell of his cologne made her head spin. Why hadn't it washed off in the rain? "I was raised to be afraid of only the devil himself," she retorted, her chin raised stubbornly.

"And?" Blake arched an eyebrow at her, looking amused.

"I think you're him." She turned her back to him again before he could see the trembling desire in her eyes.

He gave a hearty laugh. "Well, you needn't worry. I'm a nice devil. I'd never do anything you didn't want me to do, although from what I gathered out there, before we were so rudely interrupted, you do want to. I wouldn't be forcing you in the end."

"Good choice of words," she said, facing him, her eyes flashing. "The end. One tryst with you and it would be all over. No, thank you."

"How about if I promised you two trysts?" he teased, reaching out to caress her face and lips.

She was furious. He was still laughing at her, still playing games when she was deadly serious. How dare he tease her so unmercifully when inside she was torn in two, aching for his touch, yearning for his caress, but fighting herself and him with all her strength because he would never love her the way she loved him. Suddenly her frustration was too much to bear and her anger exploded. She raised her hand to strike him, but he caught it in a swift movement.

His voice was deadly serious now. "You make me out to be a bluebeard." His hard gaze trapped her.

"He was a piker compared to you," she retorted. "How many of us do you want to dangle on a string? Sheila, Rhonda, me, and who knows who else."

"Try the entire population of Phoenix," he suggested, allowing his own anger to show. "Maybe we'll throw in New York and London too!"

Her green eyes blazed. "I wouldn't be surprised."

Another crack of thunder sounded as if it were in the room with them, making Brittany jump. And then his arms went around her and his lips crushed hers, bruising her mouth with a powerful urgency, kissing her resolve away, kissing her anger to shreds, reducing her to a woman filled with unquenched desire.

"There," he said, finally lifting his mouth from hers, "that's from Bluebeard. That's what you're turning away," he told her angrily. He pushed her away from him and stalked out, slamming the door behind him. The cottage shook.

Brittany threw open the door and ran after him. "Blake!" she screamed. "Don't go out there. It's raining too hard!"

He kept walking. "The weather's better out here than it is in there," he shouted back.

She ran after him and caught up to his long strides. She seized his elbow and pulled him to a stop. "Come back inside, Blake, and wait until it stops raining," she pleaded. "There's lightning out here."

"I'm more in danger of getting fried in the cottage." The rain streamed into his eyes and he blinked to see her.

"Please, no more quarrels, no more anything, just come back inside," she begged, not letting go of his elbow.

But he pulled away again and kept walking. As he did so Brittany was caught off balance and stumbled, falling. She gasped in surprise.

Immediately he was bending over her, helping her up. "I'm sorry," he apologized, his expression filled with concern.

"I'm alright," she told him. "Just a bigger mess than I was, that's all."

She was able to stand by herself, but he swept her up in his arms with an effortless motion. Surprised, she didn't try to resist, merely wrapped her arms about his neck and buried her wet face in his shoulder, feeling the hard muscle beneath his soaked shirt. She felt as if she could stay in his arms forever.

Blake carried her inside, kicking the door shut with the heel of his shoe. He made no move to relinquish her as he gazed down into her face.

"Aren't you going to set me down?" she asked softly, trying to keep the tremor from her voice.

"Oh, yes," he said, as if just realizing where he was. A small smile played about his lips. "You're as light as a feather. I guess I forgot I was carrying you," he confessed, his face a scarce inch away from hers.

"Some wet feather," she mumbled. Still he made no move to put her down. "The floor, Blake," Brittany reminded him, glancing down. "I'd like to feel the floor."

"Any way you want it, Sacajawea," he said with a chuckle and she knew what he meant. A deep blush colored her cheeks as he let her slip from his grasp. Why was he always twisting her words? Or did she unconsciously leave them open to his manipulation?

Abruptly she turned away from him and looked out the window. "It doesn't look like it's going to let up," she said, her throat dry.

Blake came up behind her. She felt the warmth of his skin despite their wet clothes. "No, it doesn't," he agreed softly.

Brittany turned to look at him in the fading light. He touched her cheek gently, but made no further move toward her. Instead he looked about the cabin and strode over to the cot, stripped off the large dusty blanket, and held it out to her.

"Get those wet things off and put this around you," he told her. Brittany opened her mouth in protest, but he added, almost with a touch of sadness, "I promise I won't touch you."

Her protest died unspoken as another sneeze seized her body. She shook her head.

Blake sighed. "Little Indian princess, for once I'll be a gentleman—if you promise not to tell anyone of the golden opportunity I let slip through my fingers. Now please, stop fighting me and do as I say. You have two minutes to obey."

"And if I don't?" she asked, lifting her chin defiantly.

Blake made no answer. Instead he reached out slowly and began to unbutton her blouse, his fingers burning through the light, clinging material. Brittany's first instinct was to draw back, but she stood frozen to the spot, unable to move even if her life depended on it. Slowly the blouse parted, and in the dim light appeared the firm outline of her breasts, hidden beneath the lacy bra. With a gentle motion Blake slid the blouse off her shoulders, his hands caressing every inch of skin the material touched.

Deftly he unhooked the top of her jeans and with a hand on either side, slid them over her hips until they lay in a crumpled heap on the floor. Half frightened, half anticipating something wonderful to happen, Brittany could not take her eyes off Blake's face.

"Take a step, please," he said in a voice so soft she barely heard him. But she did as bidden. He kicked the jeans off to one side and reached behind her to unfasten her bra. Her hand went out to stop him, but the effort was almost halfhearted, and Blake managed to unsnap the catch beneath her grasping fingers. The material immediately loosened in the front.

"Blake," she managed to say in protest between lips that were dry and trembling.

His eyes, a bright, mesmerizing blue that not even the dim light could hide, moved down to her face. He ceased what he was doing and reached for the blanket on the floor. Tenderly he wrapped it about her shoulders. A shiver went over her.

"Okay," he murmured into her hair. "I promised and I'll keep my promise."

Brittany was surprised. And very grateful. Suddenly a special feeling came over her and she looked at Blake with new affection and deeper trust.

Then he began to strip off his own shirt and peel off the wet, clinging jeans. Brittany's eyes widened at the sight of him.

"Don't tell me you've never seen a naked man before," he said. His tone was teasing and he seemed to be enjoying the effect he had on her.

Brittany averted her face. "I, um, Jonathan always wore pajamas and, um..." Her voice faded.

Blake came over to her and crooked his finger beneath her chin. "Okay, you keep your panties on and I'll keep mine—sound fair?" He laughed.

Brittany didn't know how to answer him. Part of her was annoyed at the fact that he was obviously laughing at her, and part of her was relieved that he had stopped when he had. Unintentionally her eyes swept over him as he stood before her in his briefs. He had a magnificent body, and her heart began to beat hard again.

Showing remarkable foresight, Blake had managed to salvage the wine when they had run for cover. They spent the evening sipping it straight from the bottle and waiting for the rain to stop. By the time it let up, it was far too dark to go anywhere. Blake lit the candles he had found. His face glowed in the small circle of light, which cast giant shadows on the walls.

"There's only one bed," he pointed out, "and one

blanket. I'm afraid we're going to have to share both."
One look at his face told Brittany he wasn't "afraid" in
the least. He was enjoying her discomfort.

"I can see that," Brittany said, trying to keep her voice
cool. "You've behaved yourself so far," she said point-
edly, her eyes intent on him.

"Yes, and hasn't it been dull?" Blake countered, the
light from the candles playing upon his powerful body,
accentuating the movement of his muscles beneath the
skin.

"No," she replied, her face softening, "it hasn't been
dull. It's been rather nice. You can be very nice when
you want to . . ."

"That's hitting below the belt," Blake told her.
"You're doing that so I'll stay good."

"Right," she admitted with a laugh.

His laugh blended with hers as he picked her up suddenly and deposited her on the bed. His long form loomed
over her. "Blanket, please."

Gingerly she unwrapped the end and rolled slightly
to give up part of the tattered covering. As she turned
to face him, she suddenly realized that her bra was still
undone and hurriedly moved to fix it.

"No," he said, reaching out to stop her. "Take it off."
He covered her breasts with part of the blanket, his hand
purposely rubbing against them as he did so. "Let me
have some concessions."

He pulled in close to her, wrapping the opposite end
of the blanket about him. His eyes spoke volumes.

chapter

8

BRITTANY FELT A warmth enveloping her as she sensed the outline of Blake's muscular body against hers. She longed to give in to the growing temptation before her and struggled to remember that she would live to regret it.

"Did he make you happy?" Blake asked suddenly. Brittany turned to look at him, his face only inches away from hers on the pillow. "Your late husband, did he make you happy in bed?"

The color rose to her cheeks. "I don't see where that's any of your business."

"Everything about you is my business. I want to know everything there is about you. Who your first-grade teacher was, what secrets you whispered into your pillow at night. I intend to be a Brittany expert," he told her. The words were less mocking than they were a gentle promise.

She was silent for a moment, wanting to confide in him but finding it difficult to voice thoughts and feelings she had never revealed to anyone. Slowly she replied, "No. He never made me happy. Resigned, perhaps, to the life I had ahead and yet . . . no, happy was an emotion I did not experience with him." She left the statement to Blake's interpretation.

He made a move toward her and the mattress shifted,

causing Brittany to fall against him. "Well, if you insist..." he teased, putting his arm about her.

"Blake!"

He held up his hands. "Look, ma, no hands." He punched the pillow beneath him. It was flat as a board. "I want you to know that this is a first for me and I'm not too crazy about it."

"I appreciate it," she murmured, settling back, somewhat less tense now.

"You'd better appreciate it. That's twice you owe your virtue to me—once for saving you from that hulk in the diner, and now from myself. You owe me, lady," Blake repeated as his eyes closed.

Brittany lay watching him in the flickering candlelight, waiting for him to move toward her, half afraid he would, half afraid he wouldn't. But he seemed to have fallen asleep. Slowly she relaxed her tense muscles, gradually letting her guard down, feeling utterly exhausted. Within minutes she was fast asleep.

She awoke once during the night to find herself curled up against Blake, fitting intimately against the curve of his body. He had thrown one arm about her, and as she listened to his even breathing, she was assured that he was still asleep. Feeling safe, she allowed herself the luxury of enjoying the warmth of his body and the sense of being so terribly close to him.

A long time later, still half asleep, she moved her hand restlessly across the bed where he had been lying. Her fingers met empty space and her eyes flew open as she came abruptly awake. She found Blake standing over her, fully dressed, a big grin on his face. He was doing up the last buttons on his shirt and tucking it into his pants.

"Get up, sleepyhead," he greeted her. "Time to get up and go home."

Brittany bolted upright, than grabbed the blanket that had fallen away, exposing her perfect breasts. Blake's bold gaze covered every inch of her before she rearranged the covering.

He chuckled at her modesty. "Too late," he said lightly. "I've memorized every curve of your delectable flesh." Brittany opened her mouth but no words would come. "Get your clothes on, Sacajawea," he added. "I'll even turn around for you."

But as she slipped out of bed he peeked over his shoulder.

"Blake, you promised—"

"Don't trust me, do you?" He chuckled again.

"With good reason."

"Madam, you wound me to the quick. Wasn't I good last night?"

"Yes, you were," she admitted. "You can turn around now. Thank you, Blake," she said softly, kissing his lips lightly. "Thank you for not taking advantage."

"Don't remind me," he said.

She ran her hand over his stubby chin. "I'm not used to seeing you with a five o'clock shadow." Her eyes shone with amusement.

"How do I look?"

"A little like a pirate," she told him saucily.

"If I were a pirate, I would have given you a choice of me or walking the plank last night, instead of lying there like a meek eunuch."

"You did a very nice thing," she persisted.

He opened the door, not commenting. "Ready? We've got a long walk ahead of us." She nodded and preceded him outside.

It was a beautiful day, still early enough in the morning to be cool, but late enough to be sunny. There wasn't a cloud in the sky, and after the recent rain the air smelled fresh and clean. Brittany took a deep breath and stretched up on her tiptoes. For some reason it felt wonderful to be alive. Being with Blake filled her with happiness.

They set off at a brisk pace, but less than half a mile down the trail they found both their horses munching grass as if nothing had happened. Blake approached them cautiously and grabbed the reins of both animals, then brought them back to Brittany.

"Miserable creatures," he commented dryly. "I thought they'd be halfway back to the house by now."

"Don't insult them," Brittany said, swinging easily into the saddle. "Without them we'd be tired and aching by the time we got home. What are you grinning at?" she demanded, just then seeing his expression.

"Do you know you talk in your sleep?" he asked as they headed the horses toward home.

Brittany was aghast. "What did I say?" she asked cautiously.

"Mostly 'no, Blake.' Am I on your mind that much?"

She tried to shrug nonchalantly. "Well, considering the circumstances, it would seem odd if you weren't."

"I see," Blake said. She felt he was mocking her, but she smiled. Whatever else, when necessary he was a gentleman. She felt a sunny warmth spread all through her. Maybe he did care for her just a little after all.

Etienne was the first to see them as they entered the front door, and he took long strides past the butler to get to them first. "Where have you two been?" he demanded.

"Waiting out the storm in that old deserted cottage," Blake told him. "Got anything ready to eat? We're starved."

Etienne looked the two of them over, making Brittany feel like a bedraggled rat. Her clothes were wrinkled and slightly soiled, and her hair hung limply about her shoulders.

"Are you alright?" Etienne asked, obviously suspicious of Blake's treatment of her.

"Just a little water-logged, but none the worse for wear," Blake answered glibly for her.

"Where the devil have you been?" they heard Ambroise roar. His wheelchair purred across the parquet floor.

"Stranded. The horses ran off and we took shelter at the cottage," Blake said, shifting from one foot to another. "We'll tell you all about it later." His discomfort amused Brittany. It was about time he suffered for his mischief-making.

"Britt?" Ambroise asked, raising an eyebrow at her.

"I'm fine," she answered. "Just hungry."

The old man waved his hand. "Go on, get dressed. The cook will have breakfast for you presently." He turned steel-blue eyes on his son and blocked Blake's way with the wheelchair. Blake looked down at him, waiting. "Is she alright?" Brittany heard Ambroise ask as she headed for the stairs. She stopped to look back.

"I left her as I found her," Blake informed him. "I'm not the total scoundrel you take me for, dad. Now, if you'll excuse me, I need a shower." Together he and Brittany ascended the stairs.

Another week went by in which Brittany had little contact with Blake, and then, rather abruptly, she came to the end of Elizabeth's journal.

I have been accepted back into society rather tenuously. Amos Kincade proposed marriage to me, allowing that he would adopt my son as his own. He is a kind man. I have no choice. I do not care about myself, for at twenty-three I have lived the better part of my life and have no right to expect any more. But my son, my son, the world is open before him, open and hostile, for he does not have the protection of a good name. Life will be hard enough for him without my denying him this. I will accept Amos, despite the fact that he is older than my father was when he died. I am fortunate.

Elizabeth certainly didn't sound fortunate, Brittany thought, fingering the yellowed paper, the last leaf in the journal. Among the papers she found a corresponding afterthought that Elizabeth had written several years later.

> I was right. Amos is a good man. I do not love him the way I did Nachise, but he meets my needs and my son thrives. I thank God each night for smiling on me. Only a little do I still ache for those brief days of happiness that came and went so quickly. Oh, Nachise.

Brittany replaced the papers in the box and sighed. Elizabeth had chosen a secure life and died without knowing physical deprivation, enjoying the love of a good man. But was that enough? Having once known passion with Nachise, had it been enough? Brittany sympathized with the plight of the woman who had died so long ago.

Her thoughts turned to Blake. He had been polite to her, had even teased her a little since the night they had spent in the cottage. But he had not gone out of his way to be with her. Suddenly she wondered why. Was it Sheila? Was there someone new? Had her refusal to make love with him finally driven him away? She felt torn between good sense and desire. Her emotions had never dominated her thoughts and actions before, but since she had come to the house—was it really only a little more than two months ago?—she had known nothing but emotional turmoil. And she had never felt so fully alive.

Putting down her pen and slipping her shoes back on, Brittany went in search of Blake. According to Etienne he'd gone to the garage soon after breakfast. She found him there, tinkering with the car he was to drive in the last—and most important—race of the season, which was two weeks away.

The garage itself, larger than most houses Brittany was acquainted with, could hold seven cars and included an area set aside for Blake and his race car. Separated from the main garage by shelves of tools, it was not unlike a mechanic's workshop, but much cleaner.

"Hi," Brittany said almost shyly. Blake turned around in surprise, a lazy smile coming to his lips.

"Hi yourself. Why are you roaming around free?" he asked. "I thought I was your only savior, unchaining you from your desk periodically so you would remember there was a world out here."

"I finished," she said.

"The whole book?" He tried to sound interested. There was grease on his face and he stood over the gaping hood of the car, looking into a mass of hoses and parts that boggled Brittany's mind as she peered over his shoulder.

"Just the interesting part—about the Indians. There's only a little more about her life afterwards," Brittany explained. "Then comes the hard part—editing and writing. I've never edited anything before except my father's sermons."

"You obviously committed some to memory too," Blake muttered under his breath. "You'll do fine," he assured her. Then he stopped and looked up at her again. "What are you doing here? I know—you missed me. I knew I'd get to you sooner or later."

Brittany felt embarrassed. "I just wanted to share my good news with someone."

"What good news?"

"That I finished the book—the good part. You weren't listening."

"I prefer to be looking," he told her, his eyes glinting with a devilish twinkle.

Brittany pulled a paper towel from a dispenser on the wall behind Blake and wiped the smudge from his nose. "Dirt doesn't belong on you," she said.

Their eyes met and held for a moment, then Brittany looked away. "You're lucky I'm messy right now," Blake told her softly.

A polite cough came from the doorway. They turned to see the butler standing there, looking a little uncomfortable. "Telephone, sir," he announced.

"Be right there. You stay here," Blake told Brittany.

She obeyed without quite knowing why and amused herself by looking over the large collection of cars. A somber-looking, navy Rolls-Royce belonged to Ambroise, and the two men shared a tan Mercedes. Then there was Blake's collection—a silver Ferrari, a blue Corvette Stingray, a mink-colored Jaguar XKE, and— Brittany's head spun when she thought of the cost of all these vehicles—the little number Blake had had built to his own specifications, his pride and joy, the race car. To her it looked like an ugly little creature, low and wide, that hugged the road as if it were one with it. It symbolized her greatest rival.

Brittany was running her hand along the sleek, polished body, wondering if the lure of the race would ever leave Blake, when she heard him mutter an oath behind her as he returned to the garage.

"What's the matter?" she asked, glancing up. He had cleaned up a little; the grease was gone from his hands and face and he had changed from the dirty coveralls he had been wearing to a pair of brown trousers and a light brown short-sleeved shirt.

"The car's supposed to be tuned up and running like a well-trained cheetah," he told her.

"So?"

"A friend just called to say my pit mechanic got himself drunk last night. He ran off to Vegas with his girl of the moment, and somewhere between the justice of the peace and the honeymoon haven, he broke his leg and is in traction in Sunrise Hospital. Damn fool."

"Will he be back in time?" Brittany asked.

"No." The word was snapped out. Blake immediately flashed her an apologetic smile.

"Can't any of your other mechanics do it?"

He shook his head. "Only the best," he muttered, deep in thought. "There's a little old man outside of Superior who works magic with his hands. He's semiretired now, but he's the only one I'd trust with this piece of machinery."

"Are you going to get him?"

Blake laughed. "You don't 'get' Doc Baker. You go to him and plead a bit and then maybe, just maybe, he'll look at your car. Orneriest old cuss you ever laid eyes on. C'mon," he said, grabbing her hand.

"Where are we going?" she demanded, following him willingly. In her present mood she would have gone anywhere with him.

"We'll get the truck and have this baby taken to him so he can work his magic before I need it."

"You're going to leave the car with him?" she asked.

"I'm also going to leave Rusty with him," Blake said, referring to one of his pitmen. "That car doesn't stay anywhere without a proper guard."

"Blake, I can't just keep picking up and going with you," Brittany protested. "I have to tell your father what I read today."

"We'll be back by bedtime," he told her. "You can tell him his story then," he said jokingly.

She didn't have a chance to say no, and she really didn't want to. Blake wanted her company again, and the thought made her warm and happy.

Before leaving, Blake arranged to have Rusty drive the truck containing his race car. He was supposed to meet them at Doc Baker's, but the pitman was late getting there, so Blake and Brittany were forced to wait out the afternoon, exploring the few shops the small town had to offer. They ate lunch in a tiny café overlooking miles of winding desert road.

"Kind of makes you feel lonely, doesn't it?" Brittany asked, gazing out the window.

Blake smiled. "I'm not lonely," he said, his hand touching hers. "If you're finished, let's go for a walk."

"Where?" she wanted to know as they left the little

restaurant. She heard the lone waitress gasp at the tip Blake had left behind, and saw a smile cross his lips. Money didn't give Blake a sense of power or self-importance. She liked that. He was generous with what he had, but not ostentatious.

"Oh, I know my way around here," he said. "There's a little creek down the road a ways. Nothing spectacular, but kind of nice and peaceful."

"This whole town's peaceful," Brittany commented as they walked. "I'm glad Rusty's late," she confided as they came to the area Blake had mentioned. "It's been a nice afternoon."

Blake smiled and leaned her against the trunk of a tall tree whose branches bowed over the stream. "Yes, it has been nice," he agreed huskily.

He was going to kiss her, she thought, and her pulse began to race in anticipation. She didn't try to ward him off. If anything, her eyes called him closer.

Blake leaned over and kissed her very slowly, the intensity of his kiss growing with each passing second. A burning sensation started in Brittany's stomach, reaching its fiery fingers further and further until all of her was aflame. Her arms went about his neck and her knees grew weak. Suddenly she was sinking down beneath Blake as he kept on kissing her. Her thoughts floated away, overpowered by his kiss and his nearness. Tell me you love me, she pleaded silently. Tell me you love me.

His hands caressed her with growing possessiveness, roaming freely over her, and Brittany felt herself steadily losing ground, her consciousness becoming less and less clear as she was consumed by the fire he created in her by his very touch. With supreme effort she tried to rally herself, recalling how she knew that, once conquered, she would cease to hold any fascination for him. She tried to sit up.

Blake pulled away from her and looked down at her oval face, taking it tenderly in one hand.

She was intensely aware of her breasts heaving against

his arm, the intimacy of the situation both thrilling her and frightening her. They were all alone.

"What are you looking at?" she asked, her breath coming in ragged gasps.

"I'm looking for my soul," he said simply. "I think you've trapped my soul in those flashing eyes of yours." He looked at her for a long, long time. "You're a tease, Sacajawea."

Brittany pulled herself up into a sitting position. "I am not a tease!" she protested hotly. "No more than you are with all your women."

"Oh, yes," Blake said with a mocking smile. "Just dripping out of my pockets."

"Be serious," she cried. "That's your problem. You're never serious."

"And you're too serious," he told her, once more kissing her full lips.

She was losing the battle, she knew it. He was going to have her right there and then on the roadside like some casual little affair. The words stung her mind. She wanted more from him, so much more.

"No," she cried, pulling free and scrambling to her feet. "You can't—not like this . . ."

Blake sighed heavily, and she could see he was fighting for control. Well, let him. This wasn't easy for her either. It would be far easier to surrender herself to him. If he only knew how badly she wanted him, wanted to make love to him, to be held in his arms. She had to fight not only him but her intense desire as well. She was so confused about him that she no longer knew what she wanted—except to have him want her as much as she wanted him, and not just for a space of time but for all eternity. She watched him to see his reaction to her latest rejection.

Blake stood up and brushed off his clothes, then looked at her, his anger subdued but not completely gone. "I left you alone in the cottage because I promised I'd never force myself on you. But you're pushing me to the limit, Brittany. Someday those kisses of yours are going to start a fire your pleas can't put out. Let's go," he said, taking her hand somewhat gruffly and leading the way back to the shop.

Rusty was already there waiting for them. Blake seemed a little tense as he took the man aside for a few words of instruction, leaving Brittany alone. Doc Baker came up behind her, chewing on the end of an unlit pipe.

"He your fella?" he asked bluntly, pointing the pipe stem at Blake.

She shook her head, not trusting her voice for fear of it breaking. No, he wasn't her "fella" and never would be. She didn't know the secret of making him hers.

When she didn't answer, Doc Baker added, "Well, iff'n he were, I'd try to talk him out of racing if I were you. He's too good to risk his neck in those tiny little cars of his."

Brittany turned to the man with new interest. At five-feet-five inches he was somewhat shorter than she was in her three-inch heels. Seeing he had a new audience, the man sat down in his rocker and leaned back, waiting for Blake to return. "Yup, too good. Did ya know he set me up?" he asked her. "Had a fire here about three years back. Never did carry no fire insurance. No use for new-fangled things like insurance. But sure coulda used it then. Blake, he come up to see me, just for a visit, mind you, and finds me living in the hotel, nothing left to my name except my neighbors' good will. One, two, three," he said, snapping his worn fingers, "he's got money coming in to me, new equipment showing up, and saying things like, pay me later, in trade. Still won't let me fix nothing for free. I grouch at him because he expects it and it's the only hobby I got, grouching at people, but he's a good one, Blake is. Never met none better. Don't like him racing," he repeated. "Don't like it at all."

Brittany was listening to him in silence, alone with her thoughts, when Blake called Doc over for consultation.

On the way home that evening she was still silent. It had grown dark and they were traveling back to Tatum Canyon with the lights of the freeway about them. Finally Brittany said, "Mr. Baker thinks the world of you."

Blake looked at her for the first time since they'd started back. "He runs off at the mouth a bit at times," he said, shrugging. "But he's a nice old man for all his yelling. He doesn't have a family. I've kind of adopted him, I guess. Everyone needs someone."

Brittany looked at him in surprise. "Why Blake, what a nice thing to say."

"I'm full of nice things, in case you haven't noticed," he teased, his easy manner restored.

It started to rain, and Blake turned on the windshield wipers. Brittany watched the raindrops slide down the windshield outside the reach of the wipers and remembered the way Blake had caressed her face that afternoon. She ached for his touch now, and unconsciously her hand reached out toward his. He closed his right hand over hers, resting it against his thigh.

"Want to find another cottage and do it right this time?" he asked, his voice soft and husky, seductively low.

"Blake, you promised to have me home in time to tell your father the end of the story," she said. "That was the only way I agreed to come with you."

"You came with me because you wanted to be with me," he contradicted, suddenly pulling off the main road.

She looked at him in surprise and horror. "What are you doing?"

"I could tell you we just ran out of gas," he said, stopping the car.

"I know how to read a gas gauge," she reminded him.

"So why can't you read what's in my eyes?" he demanded. "It's plainer than any gas gauge. I want you, Brittany. Not for some little toss-away affair like you're thinking. You've seen too many soap operas giving us rich folk a bad name."

"I never watch soap operas," she told him. "And that has nothing to do with it. I judge from the facts."

"The facts are, Brittany, that you make my blood rush and you're driving me absolutely crazy. I'm not asking you to throw away your life. I'm asking you to be a woman, to give in to yourself." She opened her mouth to respond, but he wouldn't let her. "To give in to me. Take a little pity on me, O minister's daughter. I need you." He kissed her cheek, and began a network of kisses over every inch of her face, his hands massaging her shoulders and down her arms. He was seeking her out, making an ally out of her body, which had turned so totally against her.

In spite of herself her breath quickened and her resistance began to melt as the onslaughter of his kisses grew to a fever pitch. His hands slipped inside her shirt and he touched her in that way of his, making her ache to be his alone. His fingers glided over her flesh, feeling unbelievably tender, stroking her until she thought she would scream. So what if making love to him went against everything she had ever been taught to believe in. He was right. She wanted him as much as he wanted her. Her mind drunk with desire, Brittany reached out and took him closer in her arms, her hands clutching at his thick hair.

Suddenly a light shone into the car, making them jump apart.

"Everything all right in here?" came a booming voice. Blake looked into the flashlight of a highway patrolman. "I saw your car pulled over to the side. Lots of accidents in these sudden showers. You folks need any help?"

Yes, I do, Brittany wanted to say. She pulled herself over to the far side of the Mercedes, which offered more space than the sports car Blake usually drove.

"No, we're alright. Everything seems to be working fine now," Blake told the policeman amiably.

Brittany was amazed at how in control he sounded. He looked cool and calm, and the fact disturbed her greatly. How could he evoke such passion within her and not look the way she felt? Because it was a casual affair to him, despite all his smooth words, and she was just fooling herself if she thought anything different. Yes, he was good and kind and helpful to people, but he was unattainable in the last analysis, and she was a fool if she thought she could hold him by giving in and making love to him. He belonged to the breed of men who were forever charming, forever free of the shackles of marriage. All she would have in the end were empty dreams.

Right now she still had her pride, she told herself, and that would see her through somehow. Passion wasn't everything. Hadn't she led a perfectly satisfactory life as Jonathan's wife without it? No, she was lying to herself. Life with Jonathan had been a stifling existence. She had always felt there was something missing, something just beyond her reach. She had seen no swirling lights, felt no fiery passion the way she did now with Blake.

Blake glanced over at her as the policeman returned to his car. "Sacajawea," he said in a light, bantering tone, his good mood restored, "you have more guardian angels than any other person I know. You've got the weather and the state police on your side. I know when I'm licked—for tonight. That policeman isn't going to leave until we get started. You've won again," he told her, starting up the car. "Let's go home."

chapter

9

WHEN THEY ENTERED the house they met Ambroise, looking annoyed. "Where have you been?" he asked sharply, directing his question at his son.

"Up around Superior, seeing about a tune-up for my car. We got delayed," he said with a pleasant smile. "I'm home before midnight, dad," he added, mimicking a teenager.

"Might have known it was your fault," the older man said gruffly. "And don't give me any of your sass."

"Mr. Kincade, I'm sorry," Brittany said, interrupting what could become an argument. "I know I was supposed to be here by dinner—"

Ambroise held up his hand. "Not your fault he keeps dragging you around to parts unknown. It's just that there was someone at dinner I wanted you to meet. But don't worry," he added, turning his wheelchair around and heading back toward his den. "He'll be back tomorrow night," he promised with an air of mystery.

Who could Ambroise possibly want her to meet? Brittany wondered as she prepared for bed that night. It was the only thought she had that didn't concern Blake. Images of him plagued her all night as she tried to fall asleep but couldn't. The evening had stirred up too many

emotions and desires, and the frustration made her restless. She punched the pillow to no avail. The soft lump
refused to assume the position she wanted.

Darn Blake anyway, she thought miserably. Why did
he have to come into her life? Why didn't Mr. Kincade
have a daughter, or a cat? She wanted a wedding, a
wedding with all the trimmings. No, not necessarily a
wedding, she amended. She wanted... she wanted
Blake, that's what she wanted. She wanted his promise,
his trust, his love... But he seemed to be incapable of
making a lasting commitment of any kind. And she could
accept nothing less.

Confused and uncertain, Brittany tossed and turned
far into the night.

The next day she forced herself to put aside all tur-
bulent thoughts of Blake and go to work. She hammered
diligently away at the new typewriter Etienne had produced for her to make the project go faster. Unfortunately, it responded to the slightest touch and, until she
got used to it, she found herself typing words she had
never intended to appear on the page. Somewhere in the
back of her mind she remembered her interview months
before with Mr. Simmons, the employment agent, and
his question as to whether she typed. Her answer had
been "a little." It should have been "horribly."

Brittany's efforts became an experience in frustration.
Even the kerchief she wore around her neck, which she'd
tied so jauntily that morning, was beginning to wilt beneath her hard concentration. At lunchtime, when she
refused to budge from mastering the too-quick keys,
Etienne brought her a bite to eat. He came again at five.

"All slaves are duly freed until tomorrow," he told
her dryly.

"But I'm not anywhere near on schedule anymore,"
she moaned, eyeing the typewriter like an enemy.

"You'll catch up," he assured her. "Mr. Kincade and

I have great faith in you. Now you'd best get ready for dinner. The old gentleman has someone he'd like you to meet." Etienne ushered her out.

There was that mysterious "someone" again. "Who, Etienne?" she asked.

"I wouldn't dream of spoiling the surprise. You'll just have to wait," he told her, his thin lips twitching into a half smile.

Brittany found out soon enough. She put on a shell-blue sleeveless dress with tiny pearl buttons running down the front, leaving a few buttons undone above her knee. Blake smiled warmly at her as she entered the dining room. He was sipping an aperitif and talking politely with a man seated at his father's elbow.

The man didn't seem to be as tall as Blake, and he had far narrower shoulders. It was strange, Brittany thought, how she measured everyone against Blake now. The man's face seemed to belong to a person who was studious, quiet. He had a fair complexion with sandy-colored hair that was thinning slightly on top. He looked about forty or so. Was this the person Ambroise had been so anxious for her to meet? Why? she wondered, putting on a smile as she took her seat and the men turned toward her.

"Ah, Britt, I want you to meet Peter Dane," said Ambroise. "He's an editor with Darian Press, a line of very popular regional books."

"I'm acquainted with them," Brittany said.

"Oh, good. I told him about the work you were doing with my 'find,'" Ambroise went on with some pride, "and he seemed very interested."

Brittany's eyes grew a little wider. Was she being dismissed? "Oh, I see. You're going to take over this project. Mr. Kincade, I know that of late I've been a little lax in getting the job done, but that's only because your son—"

"Don't blame me," Blake interrupted, holding up a protesting hand but still smiling.

"I'm not blaming you. You didn't drag me off, but all the same, one doesn't say no to the boss's son," she said, turning an appealing gaze to Ambroise.

"You've been doing a pretty good job of it so far," Blake answered under his breath. Brittany heard him and prayed no one else did.

"It's nothing like that, Miss Sinclair," Peter Dane told her as he helped himself to a serving of the beef Stroganoff that was offered to him. "I wouldn't dream of taking it off your hands. Actually, we would be interested in seeing the finished product. Sometimes, if you'll forgive the choice of words, an amateur can approach this type of work with fresher eyes than an editor who's been doing smilar work time and again."

"Then I don't have to stop?" Brittany asked with relief.

"Absolutely not," Ambroise informed her.

"I'm glad. I've grown very attached to Elizabeth. We've spent a lot of time together, and I feel very close to her after peering into her soul the way I have."

"Yes, unedited diary-reading can be exciting," Peter Dane agreed in a polished accent whose tone noticeably lacked enthusiasm.

Blake cleared his throat slightly. "You'll forgive me, Mr. Dane, but hasn't this type of book been done to death lately?" he asked.

The other man regarded him as if he were an intellectual inferior, then smiled a bit too patly. "There have been a lot of such books published lately, yes. But in these trying times the public is hungry for the past—the authentic past—partly out of nostalgia and partly out of the need to know that times were bad before and that people managed to survive, to overcome their obstacles and to propagate." Peter Dane leaned forward and looked deeply into Brittany's eyes. "I'd like to call from time to time and see how the book is progressing."

Blake seemed to stiffen slightly at that comment, Brittany noticed. She didn't want to encourage Peter Dane, if he had anything other than the book in mind, but at the same time she wondered if Blake would finally realize how it felt being squeezed in between others, as she felt she was.

"Of course, if it's alright with Mr. Kincade," Brittany said, looking toward Ambroise to clarify which "Mr. Kincade" she meant.

"Of course, I have no objections," Ambroise said, appearing amused.

Blake looked at his father suspiciously.

"Better yet," Peter Dane continued, "Ambroise told me that Elizabeth was kidnapped by Cochise's Apaches. Why don't you go up to Fort Apache Indian Reservation and soak up the atmosphere there? It would give you a better feeling for the story."

"Well, I don't know." Brittany hesitated and cast a look toward Blake, whose face was impassive.

"I'm an expert on reservations. I could show you around," Peter offered. "To see those people living in their own element and culture is a worthwhile experience."

Brittany thought he made the people sound like museum pieces and she wasn't at all sure she liked his attitude, but perhaps she was being hasty.

"Ambroise, what do you say?" Peter asked, placing a well-manicured hand on the table between them.

Ambroise's bearded cheeks stretched into a wide smile. "It might help the work at that. Go on, Britt, soak up the culture. See what it was like for Elizabeth."

"Elizabeth didn't live on the reservation for long," Blake interjected. "She was kicked back into the white world when the Chiricahua were herded in there, remember?"

Brittany looked at him in amazement. How did he

know all that? She hadn't discussed Elizabeth with anyone except Ambroise, and she didn't think she'd even told him that particular detail. But as she looked at Blake the outline of his jaw grew a little tense and his eyes clouded over as he met her gaze with a hooded look. She turned away.

So he was angry because she was going on a trip with Peter Dane. She didn't care. Did Blake expect her to be a wallflower and merely sit about, waiting to be clutched by the hand and whisked away whenever he got lonely? Not a chance. She would do as she pleased.

The dinner conversation shifted to more general topics as the main course was replaced with dessert and coffee. Brittany found the talk pleasant. Peter Dane dominated most of it, telling them stories about his publishing experiences and about the books he had worked on. Details he related about other captured wife-slaves were especially interesting to Brittany, and the evening passed very quickly for her.

"I'm afraid I must be pushing off," Peter Dane finally said, glancing at his watch. He turned toward Brittany. "Would you take a turn about the garden with me before I leave?" he asked stiffly.

Caught off guard, she saw no way to politely refuse. She felt Blake's eyes following her as she preceded Peter out the door into the still night air. They ambled slowly along the flagstone walk.

"You know," Peter began, after remarking what a warm evening it was, "Ambroise is quite impressed with what you've done so far."

"I haven't done anything yet," Brittany disagreed modestly. "I only told him a story."

"Ah, but the ability to organize and get at the heart of the matter is no mean talent. If you're as good as Ambroise tells me you are—and he doesn't give out praise lightly—there might be a job for you on my staff.

How would you like that?" he asked, turning to look at her. "Just think, seeing the world in new and different yet time-worn ways."

"I—I don't know what to say," she stuttered, taken aback by his unexpected offer.

"Don't say anything just yet." He took her hand and patted it in a paternal gesture. "You can give me your final answer once you've finished your work here. Now, I'll be back the day after tomorrow, bright and early, and we shall begin our journey to Fort Apache, sans John Wayne." He chuckled at his own joke and took his leave.

Blake wasn't in the dining room when Brittany returned, nor in the den with Ambroise. "What did Peter say?" the older man asked in his usual blunt style.

"He offered me a job. He said that if I was as good as you said, he'd like me on his staff, doing this sort of work all the time." Brittany still wasn't sure what had just happened. Three months ago she'd been a young woman with no skills. Now people were coming to *her* offering her jobs.

"And what did you say?" Ambroise demanded.

"Nothing yet. I still have to finish Elizabeth and that's going to take a long while."

"Not that long, Britt," Ambroise commented with a meaningful look.

Confused, Brittany studied the old man for a moment. It was almost as if he was trying to throw Peter and her together to get rid of her. She didn't know what to make of it.

"If you'll excuse me, I think I'll turn in early," she said, seeking the solitude of her bedroom.

The next morning Brittany changed her mind about going to the reservation with Peter Dane. True, she wanted to see the people and take in a little of what Elizabeth must have lived through, but she wanted to do it on her own. This wasn't the time to bring another man into her life, even if Peter was only interested in her for professional reasons.

Brittany ran into Ambroise as she was walking about the garden path, deep in thought. "Lovely morning, Britt," he greeted her. "For once the sun hasn't roasted everything in sight. First time in a week the temperature hasn't hit a hundred by this time of day. No, no," he said as she stopped. "Keep walking. I can keep up." She smiled in agreement but slowed her pace to match the speed of his wheelchair. "I liked the pages you left with me last night," he added. "You have a flair for wording things, Britt."

"Oh, it's not me, it's Elizabeth," she protested, stopping abruptly in her tracks as she recognized the two figures standing in front of the main door. The flash of Sheila's platinum-blond hair caught her eye just as Blake's solid outline became distinguishable. Ambroise stopped his wheelchair, which allowed Brittany to catch most of what was being said.

"Now I won't take no for an answer," Sheila was saying. "I want a little spin in your cute little car. I had one of those stupid boys you keep around to take care of the cars bring it out. I just love the XKE. Oh, please, Blakey," she pleaded in a girlish voice. Although she was too far away to see, Brittany could imagine her provocative pout, the vivid red lips turning down in a sad frown. "You've been keeping yourself away from everything," Sheila continued. "All your friends are beginning to think you don't like them anymore. Now there's a party at Arthur's this afternoon and if we hurry we can make it." She was climbing into the car. "C'mon, darling. There's room for two," she coaxed. "Of course, it's kind of tight, but I love being in little spaces with you."

Brittany became conscious that she was chewing the

inside of her lip with nervous irritation. It took supreme self-control to keep herself from actually running over and pulling the woman out of the car by her hair. But when she saw Blake get in next to Sheila, her anger turned to pain and she felt something die inside. She didn't hear what he said to Sheila. All she knew was that Blake had driven off with Sheila—again. She fought hard to keep the hurt she felt out of her voice as her gaze followed the departing vehicle.

"Mr. Kincade, I'd like to call Mr. Dane and tell him that I'm available this afternoon if he wants to get an early start," she told Ambroise. "We can arrive at Fort Apache by tomorrow morning."

With that she walked back inside the house and up to her room to be alone with her hurt. Blake hadn't told her he didn't want her to go off with another man. Indeed, he seemed to take it as a signal to go back to his old ways—if he had ever left them—to go back to his party circuit with Sheila. Maybe he was even relieved that Peter Dane had appeared when he had, to take her, Brittany, off his hands. Suddenly enraged, Brittany yanked off her shoes and threw them against the wall. But the act did nothing to assuage her grief. Finally she sank down on the bed and cried.

Etienne knocked on her door half an hour later to inform her that Peter could not be located. Their plans stood as originally arranged. Brittany decided there was nothing left to do except go back to work. Perhaps transcribing Elizabeth's journals would help her forget her confusing thoughts and problems.

Blake returned a few hours later, but it didn't occur to Brittany that he was back early. It didn't even occur to her that she should stop and return his greeting as she accidently passed him in the hall on her way back to her room. Her head was splitting and she just wanted to get to her room and lie down.

"Hey, didn't you hear me?" Blake asked when she failed to respond.

She turned on her heel, fire in her eyes. "Why don't you go crawl into a little space?" she demanded, referring to Sheila's earlier comment.

"What?" he asked, not understanding her.

"Never mind," she said, waving him out of her way. "I have work to do," she added angrily.

"You're going in the wrong direction," he called after her. "Hey," he cried, a large smile spreading across his lips, "are you jealous, Sacajawea?"

"To be jealous I'd have to care," she spat out.

"Yes, you would, wouldn't you?" Blake caught her upper arm and pulled her around into his arms. He kissed her fiercely then looked deeply into her eyes. "Yes, you would," he repeated softly.

She pushed him away, tired and angry. "Get away from me. Didn't you get enough from your friend?"

"I went to a party and saw a few friends," he told her evenly, then his own temper began to rise. "And don't get so high and mighty with me, Brittany. I'm not the one going off to the reservation with Dane, you are. Is that the type of man you're saving yourself for?"

"You insufferable egotist," she shouted at him. "That's all anything boils down to, isn't it? I'm saving myself, for your information, for a man who will love me, not a playboy who wants to seduce every woman he sees!"

"Well, maybe Dane is right for you then. He lives in the past too. The two of you can hold hands and shy away from life together!" He turned angrily on his heel and strode down the hall to his own room.

Brittany felt drained from the anger inside her. Forgetting whose house she was in, she slammed the door to her room, then fell across the bed, too tense to sleep, too hurt to cry.

* * *

Brittany ate breakfast early the next morning, hoping to avoid meeting Blake at the table. Peter arrived shortly thereafter, driving up in a large El Dorado. She dropped her overnight case onto the back seat, then slid into the plush cream-colored seat next to Peter and relaxed.

"I've taken the liberty of making reservations for us at the local hotel in the town of Fort Apache," he told her. She nodded absently, her mind elsewhere—on Blake—despite her best efforts not to think about him. She would rather be spending the time with him. What a fool she was, she cried silently.

"Have you been in this business long?" Brittany asked, determined to be polite. She watched the countryside speed past the window.

"Oh, some fifteen years or so, I daresay. It's been one long love affair with my work, so I'm not counting years. There's something very rewarding about delving into the past of a land as great as ours."

Brittany warmed to the subject somewhat and time passed quickly as they made their way to Fort Apache, located east of Phoenix. She felt relaxed in Peter's company. There was no tension between them, no charged excitement the way there was with Blake. So why wasn't she really enjoying herself? Why did she keep longing for Blake?

They arrived at the hotel late that morning. Brittany's room was small and cramped and reminded her of her old room at the parsonage. How far she'd come and how much she'd done in such a short time, she marveled. Three months ago everything in her life had been in perfect order. She had had a firm position in the community, helping her husband the way she had helped her father before him. Everything had been preplanned, predictable—and boring, she reflected. And now she was experiencing emotions totally alien to her and totally wonderful. But the old Brittany still existed, for she wanted to marry Blake, not just have a passing fling.

Brittany left her room and went down the hall to knock on Peter's door. He joined her in a few minutes, and they got back in the car, ready for a full day of sight-seeing. Later they toured some of the terrain on foot. Peter kept up an informative if somewhat dry description of what they were seeing and why it was significant. His talk left Brittany vaguely dissatisfied. She wanted to see the land—to experience it—as Elizabeth had seen and experienced it. Brittany would have preferred to be alone, just as Elizabeth had been alone, a single white woman thrust into an alien culture. But Peter thought his way of seeing the land was best, and Brittany didn't argue with him.

Peter took her out to dinner that night and, although the conversation was interesting, Brittany's thoughts kept wandering off, recalling moments she had shared with Blake. Even here, with another man at her side who was attentive and every bit a gentleman, her thoughts were only of Blake. She must stop this preoccupation with him, she told herself sternly. The project would end soon and she would probably accept Peter's offer. After all, she had little more choice than Elizabeth had had. Security counted for something. She might find another job elsewhere, but she mustn't under any circumstances hang onto Blake. He'd soon grow tired of her the way he'd grown tired of so many other women before her.

"You look far away," Peter commented pleasantly when she suddenly realized he was asking her a question. "Am I boring you with all this shop talk?"

"Oh no, no, I'm sorry. I was just thinking of all these people living out their lives on this little plot of land," she lied neatly.

"It's hardly little," he told her. "I've known of game preserves that were smaller, and animals do need more space to roam about than people do."

"Do they?" she asked dryly.

"Besides, this is the only way the Indians are able to keep the land of their ancestors."

"This was all the land of their ancestors once," she corrected him.

Peter merely smiled. "My, you do feel for these people, don't you? I really hope you'll consider my offer about coming to work for me. You'll add fresh color to the company, not to mention the fact that you will decorate it quite nicely."

She recognized his flattery for what it was, but let it go. "I am considering your job offer," she told him simply. "I'm giving it a great deal of consideration." The fact did not give her any pleasure.

Peter smiled and his hand brushed lightly against hers. "That makes me quite happy."

She smiled back a bit stiffly. She needed a job so she would have to be pleasant, she told herself. But she didn't care for Peter's views on the Apaches and she didn't know if they came from bigotry or ignorance. Whatever the source, she found she had no patience with him. She knew why she felt so restless and dissatisfied, and she chided herself for it. Blake belonged to another world, just as Nachise had for Elizabeth. Elizabeth had enjoyed five years with her love and produced a son with him, while she herself had had only a few months and an unfulfilled romance with Blake. But the end would be the same. The world Peter offered her, the world of the single working woman, was the one she belonged to now. She would have to make the best of it.

When they returned to the hotel there was a message waiting for Peter, asking him to call his office right away. It was late, so he waited until the next morning and was rewarded with a great piece of news.

"They've made some sort of new discovery," he explained to Brittany over breakfast. "I can't talk about it now, but they want me back right away. I'm sorry, but we'll have to cut our visit short."

"That's alright, I'll stay on alone," she assured him. "I'd like to learn a little more."

"Alone?" he asked, incredulous.

She smiled with genuine pleasure for the first time since they'd begun the trip. "Yes, I like doing things alone. Don't worry about me," she added, sipping her coffee. Suddenly she felt free and excited.

Dressed in comfortable jeans and a white shirt with rolled-up sleeves, Brittany began her own tour of the reservation without the benefit of a paid guide. She wandered about wherever she was allowed to go, talking to people and absorbing the scenery. She found regular homes, to be sure, but also tipis, some for the benefit of tourists and some for the Indians who would not give up the old ways, rebelling against the white world that was trying to swallow them up.

Brittany passed several women sitting outside the tipis, making dried corn necklaces or weaving blankets to sell. They looked happy enough, she thought. One young girl smiled at her and Brittany returned the smile until the girl's mother told her to get back to work, reminding Brittany that the necklaces and blankets were a main source of income.

Several men on horses passed Brittany as they rode out to move their cattle to other grazing land. They looked like any other cowboys. Perhaps life here wasn't so bad for them either, she thought.

Brittany spent the whole day on her own, riding a palomino she had rented, feeling calm and serene under the great blue sky, at one with her surroundings. It was truly a beautiful country. But even here her thoughts eventually returned to Blake, robbing her of peace. Who was he with now? she wondered more than once. Try as she might, she had as little control over the direction

of her thoughts now as she had over her emotions when
Blake was with her.

The following day, dressed more or less the same
way, Brittany got another early start. As she walked out
of the hotel room toward the stable to get her horse, she
felt the dry heat of the day already taking hold. It was
going to be another hot one, she thought, missing the
air-conditioned comfort of the Kincade mansion. She
smiled briefly. It wasn't really the air-conditioning she
missed, and she knew it.

The stable owner had the palomino already saddled
and waiting for her. Taking the bridle, she led the horse
outside. As she swung into the saddle, she suddenly
realized she wasn't alone. Startled, she turned to see
Blake astride a big black stallion, a wide grin splitting
his face. He looked resplendent in form-fitting jeans and
a bright yellow shirt, of which the first three buttons
were open, showing a significant expanse of chest.

"What—what are you doing here?" Brittany stuttered,
stunned but pleased. If only her heart would stop pounding so hard. She was sure he must have heard it. She
tried to remind herself that she was angry with him, but
she couldn't contain her happiness.

"I didn't want you running around by yourself.
Thought you might get lonely," he said easily.

"How did you know I was alone?" Her eyes narrowed
as a sudden idea came to her. "You did that! You had
Peter called back!" she exclaimed.

"He must have arrived in Tombstone by now," Blake
told her, a lazy smile curling his lips.

"Well, of all the gall! I won't let you get away with
it," she told him, turning her horse toward the reservation. "I rather like being alone," she called over her
shoulder, but already a smile was creeping into her voice.

"If you don't let me tag along, I'll yell discrimina-
tion," Blake warned her, his horse falling into place next
to hers.

"Against who? Rich people?" she scoffed.

"No, against Indians. There is that Indian blood in me, you know," he reminded her. "And you never can tell what these Apaches might do to avenge a fellow tribesman. They might even burn you at the stake."

"Alright, alright," she said, giving in. "You can come."

Their eyes met and locked and Brittany couldn't help returning his smile.

They rode northwest toward Cedar Creek, where Elizabeth had camped most of the time during her captivity. It was beautiful country. After several hours they dismounted on a bluff high above the trees. Brittany sighed. It was like an enchanted land. And it had seen so much. It was hard to believe that men had once fought and died here to keep what was theirs, to avenge slain comrades, and to wreak havoc on the encroaching white world.

A warm breeze stirred up feelings of excitement within her. Whether it was due to where she was or whom she was with she wasn't sure.

Blake had said very little during the ride. She looked at him now, wondering what was going on in his head. "Why did you send Peter away?" she asked without preamble, suddenly needing to know.

"So I could be alone with you," he told her simply, playing with a strand of her long hair. "I don't like anyone who takes you away from me." He was serious and she waited for him to say more, but he changed the subject and his tone. "So, what do you think of it so far?" he asked.

She looked out across the river at the tall pines. "I feel for these people. It all seems so unfair, telling them they should live on these little plots of land."

"They're free to leave," he reminded her, sitting down on the ground at her feet.

She looked down at him. "Yes, they're free to go

places where they're almost sure to encounter a lot of prejudice. Do you realize that until just a little while ago there were places that had signs in their windows saying, 'No dogs or Indians allowed'? In that order." She clenched her fists. "Everyone remembers the painted red devils. Nobody remembers Wounded Knee or dozens of other massacres of Indians by whites. They don't remember the policy of extermination that was implemented by the government for over thirty years. They don't remember all the treaties broken by the white man or the fact that Custer's last stand was the result of his own egomania. He sought out the Sioux, who had permission to be off the reservation hunting food for the winter. Custer wanted to force an attack so he could become a national hero and ease his way into the presidency the way Grant had done with the Civil War."

"You can come down now," Blake told her, taking hold of her clenched fist. "There's no need to stand on a soapbox with me, bombarding me with what I already know."

"You do?" she asked, sinking down beside him. She looked at him in surprise.

"Unbeknownst to my father and unheralded by the world, I've been to this reservation before and I do know a little about Indians. Even though I didn't know Sacajawea was a Shoshoni," he added with a smile. "You don't have to convince me the Indians got a raw deal."

"The fact that they still keep getting one is the problem," she said. "The past, good or bad, is dead and should be left as such by the white world. But the Indians of today should be evaluated as individuals, not as aliens assigned to an allotted piece of land. Do you realize that they were the last people to become citizens of their own land?"

Blake touched her face fondly and she knew the familiar thrill that raced through her. "You sound like a crusader," he murmured.

"I do, don't I?" She smiled ruefully. "I just wish I could do something."

"Someday the bridge will be gapped and people will understand. People are people in the final analysis. They cry, they bleed, they live and die. And love." He whispered the last word.

Brittany wondered if he was trying to tell her something. She waited, sitting very still, her upturned face cupped in his strong, gentle hands. He studied her for a long while.

"I don't like arguing, Brittany," he finally said softly.

"We're not arguing now." She kept her eyes down.

He lowered his hands to her waist. "Not now, but at the house. We can spend our time together in so much more pleasant ways." He kissed her temple and her pulse quickened.

"You were the one who started it," she reminded him with effort.

"You were going off with Dane to see the reservation."

"Not every man tries to seduce me," she told him.

"How many have there been?" he asked softly, kissing her brow, then the tip of her nose.

"None until you," she answered truthfully, her voice husky. Not even Jonathan. He had never laid a hand on her until after they were married, and even then there had been no explosions of colored lights, no waves of heat the way there were now. It had all been so plain.

"Then everyone else is a fool," Blake told her, his lips brushing against her cheek fleetingly, but arousing such passion within her that she could hardly stand it. Every fiber of her body cried out for more.

"Blake, don't," she murmured, wondering how she found the strength to say the word.

"No, not this time, Brittany. I won't listen." He took the hands that feebly attempted to push him away. "Brittany, I want to be more than friends. I can't take this anymore. Every time I see you, whatever words we're saying, all I can think of is having you, holding you in my arms and kissing you until I break down that damn wall you've built between us. It's not natural, Brittany. I can tell you want me."

He kissed away the words of protest from her lips, flooding her in a river of kisses that sent her wits reeling away. Yes, she wanted him, wanted him more than anything in her life. Nothing mattered except that he had her in his arms and wanted her too.

Brittany felt his lips working their way downward, kissing the side of her neck, the hollow of her throat, the area exposed by her cotton blouse. She felt his hands on her, caressing her shoulders, her arms. All the while he was murmuring words of endearment to her. She was on fire as she squeezed her eyes tight against flashes of colors that exploded in her head. He was undoing the buttons of her blouse, his fingers and then his lips caressing her lightly. There was nothing left in her with which to fight him off any longer. Yes, she wanted him. Yes!

Just then the horses whinnied excitedly. The noise penetrated Brittany's consciousness with difficulty. Blake raised his head to look in their direction. At the sound of approaching hoofbeats her mind suddenly snapped to attention. Her hands flew to her half-opened blouse and quickly rebuttoned it. She pushed her hair off her face.

The rider approaching them was an Indian dressed in Western clothing. Only the headband worn across his forehead suggested his Indian heritage. A smile creased his deeply tanned face.

"You folks wander off the trail?" he asked pleasantly. "Most people don't come up around here."

Blake rose and helped Brittany to her feet. "My friend wanted to see Cedar Creek," he explained.

"Just as long as everything's alright," the Indian said, turning his horse around. "See you." He was gone in a cloud of dust.

"First time the cavalry was ever rescued by the Indians," Blake said dryly. Brittany couldn't help but smile. She felt a sense of relief, but also a pang of sorrow, which she shut her mind to.

"C'mon, I'll treat you to lunch," she said glibly.

"There's only one treat I want for lunch," he told her, but he was smiling as he mounted his horse and followed her back to the hotel.

chapter

10

BLAKE TOOK BRITTANY to dinner and held her hand as they walked back to the hotel. Not once did he suggest that they share a room. He left her at her door with a burning kiss on her lips.

Now, alone in her room, she found herself wishing the evening had not ended so quickly. "Get hold of yourself, Brittany," she ordered her image in the mirror as she brushed her ash-blond hair, which fell in heavy waves over her shoulders onto her new aqua negligee and matching robe. She hadn't known what made her pack it, but lately she'd enjoyed wearing the soft, pretty clothes Etienne had chosen for her. They made her feel desirable.

"Desirable to whom?" she murmured aloud to the mirror. "The coyotes?" She sighed and shook her head. She was losing ground rapidly in the battle against Blake, and she knew it. Even when he wasn't there to break down her defenses, her memories of him had the same effect.

Trying not to think about him further, she slipped out of the gauzelike robe and slid into bed. But she couldn't sleep. Blake haunted her every thought. As she recalled their moments together, she realized that her thoughts and attitudes toward him were changing, shifting ever so gradually. She felt a new tension, a sense that they must resolve their feelings for each other very soon or it would be too late.

Shortly her work on Elizabeth's journals would be finished and she would have to leave the Kincade home, leave Blake...forever. And although she knew she would never fit into his world and that she must get another job—perhaps accept Peter Dane's offer—she couldn't bear the thought of leaving him altogether, without first expressing her love for him. Even Elizabeth had had a brief time of passion with Nachise and had born a son to remind her of their love. But she, Brittany, had nothing except a few pleasant memories and an unfulfilled yearning. She had been saying no for so long. Now she longed to shout yes, yes, yes!

Suddenly everything she had been taught to believe meant nothing to her. She felt drawn to Blake by a wellspring of love that felt good and right. She loved him! And she had to tell him, had to show him—no matter what the consequences.

Brittany jumped out of bed and shrugged back into her robe, closing it with only one button beneath her high breasts. Her heart was pounding and her pulse racing with both fear and anticipation. What if he rejected her lovemaking, as she had so often rejected his? But no, she decided, Blake wanted her as much as she wanted him. He'd proven himself a gentleman, sensitive to her wishes, many times over. He would respond to her this time, too, but this time she wouldn't pull back at the last minute. She wouldn't deny him—and herself—the final pleasure. She wanted all of him—for just this one night—and she knew he wouldn't refuse her.

Brittany tiptoed out of her room and down the hallway to Blake's room, then tapped lightly on the door. At first there was no answer and her hopes plummeted. Then his voice called, "Who is it?"

"It's Brittany," she replied softly, her voice barely above a whisper. Immediately the door opened and he stood before her wearing a terry-cloth robe. His clear blue eyes ran down the length of her scantily clad figure, lingering on the curves of her breasts, shining with appreciation and desire. As if in a trance Brittany walked past him into the room and turned to face him, her own eyes soft with passion. Without taking his gaze off her, Blake closed the door and waited for her to speak.

She stood alone in the center of the room, suddenly unable to say the words she longed to tell him. Her heart was twisting with anguish and, to her dismay, tears filled her eyes.

"What is it?" Blake asked tenderly, stepping forward and gathering her into his arms, holding her close in his powerful embrace. He caressed her soft hair. "What is it?" he repeated.

His gentle concern melted her last defenses. "I love you," she whispered softly into his shoulder. She pulled away and met his gaze straight on. "I love you and I want to make love to you—for this one night."

His eyes never wavered from her face. "Are you sure, Brittany?" he demanded huskily. "This time I won't stop, no matter what you say."

For an answer she pressed her trembling body against his, wrapping her arms tightly around his neck, and kissed him full on the lips. With a muffled groan he crushed her closer and kissed her back. Then, with a self-control that equaled any she'd shown before, he held her away from him. His eyes devoured her, moving slowly over the soft aqua negligee that barely hid the supple body beneath it. He reached out to touch her breasts, which were straining against the lacy material.

Ever so carefully Blake slipped the robe off her shoulders, allowing it to fall in a delicate heap on the floor at her feet. The light that shone behind Brittany outlined her form as she stood before him, her legs slightly parted. In the same languid movement he gently caressed the skin beneath her breasts, running his hands slowly up over her nipples, which hardened at his touch, and then toward her throat. His fingers shot flames of heat through her and she trembled. His hands cupped her face as he drew her near and kissed her lovingly, then more and more deeply, with mounting urgency.

Brittany found herself drawn tightly into his arms, his body hard against hers. She was spinning away from the real world into a new dimension, into a world of their own creation. Nothing else mattered now but her desire to be one with him, united in pleasure.

"Oh, Blake," she moaned as he lifted her and placed her on the bed. The desire in her own eyes seemed to spur him on as he quickly shed his robe. In an instant he was covering her body with his own again, his mouth scorching hers as his hand slipped beneath the gossamerlike nightgown and found her body, caressing it, slipping tenderly and possessively over her flesh, claiming every inch as his own. In a motion that was almost rough he raised the gown over her head. She lay naked beneath him. Brittany's joy and excitement grew with every movement of his body against hers, with every touch of his hand so swiftly exploring her willing flesh. He covered her with kisses, beginning with her eyes, her cheeks, her throat, then descending to each breast, teasing her until she cried out with satisfaction.

Surprising herself, Brittany greedily explored his own muscular form, which thrilled her so. She caressed the hard muscles of his back and ran her fingers through the hair matting his chest. Her hand trailed lower, over his smooth, taut stomach, and then lower still. He groaned with pleasure, and her thrill at exciting him defied description.

Together their passion built to unimagined heights, swelling within them until they could wait no longer. Finally Blake possessed her with a gentle fury that sent her senses reeling. Suddenly she was gripped by an explosion, a release unlike anything she had ever imagined.

Flushed and trembling, she fell quiet in his arms.

"You were beautiful," he murmured against her ear as she lay enveloped in a comforting haze, the feel of his arms branding her as his own forever.

"I love you," she murmured. "I love you." And, despite her happiness, she was acutely aware that he had never said the same to her.

Brittany awoke to find the sun shining in the window. She hadn't meant to fall asleep. She had wanted to savor and relive every moment she had experienced, but sleep had claimed her at last.

Her thoughts turning to Blake, she looked to find the space next to her empty, a note propped up on the pillow. "See you at breakfast, Blake."

Immediately she felt the sting of rejection. Was it over so soon? Was she just the conquered prize and nothing more? No, she told herself, no. After all they had shared, Blake must feel something more for her. But deep in her heart she felt she had known all along that he would leave her once he had loved her.

Trying to recapture the feelings Blake had inspired in her the night before, Brittany returned to her room, where she washed and dressed. Downstairs she met a smiling Blake. His obvious good mood did much to restore her spirits.

"I have a surprise for you," he announced. "Number one, I'm taking you to some tribal dances being performed by the Apaches to entertain you white tourists," he said with a grin. "And two, there's someone here you might be interested in meeting."

Brittany could hardly contain her curiosity, but Blake refused to explain further during breakfast. Instead he talked with enthusiasm about the reservation and the Indians who lived there. Brittany realized he knew more than she had suspected earlier, and she listened with rapt attention, relieved to keep her mind off the significance

of their having made love the night before. At least Blake
still seemed to enjoy her company. He wasn't going to
leave her right away.

They attended the dances that morning. Full of religious significance, they were colorful and moving. Brittany and Blake stayed for the ceremony afterward and
also heard several of the ritual songs that had been handed
down through the generations. The Apaches had songs
to guide them through war, free them from disease, pro-
mote a good marriage, and speed a swift and brave death.
As she listened to the songs, Brittany felt closer to Elizabeth than ever before.

Blake draped his arm around her shoulders as they
watched and listened. She looked up at his profile and
thought how noble he looked. Perhaps she was imagining
it, but she thought she could see his Indian heritage in
his strong, firm jawline and high cheekbones.

The Apache warriors retreated as the ceremony concluded.

"Ready?" Blake asked and she nodded, almost sorry
to see the dances end. Once they had held deep significance for the Indian braves who danced them. Elizabeth
had watched them when the call to Usen, the Apache
deity, had been urgent and real. Now the dances repre-
sented little more than a sample of Apache culture.

Blake took Brittany's hand and led her to the last tepee
in the group. He instructed her to enter and go to the left
of the tepee after he had entered and gone to the right,
according to Apache custom. Blake sat down cross-
legged in front of a wizened old woman who was sitting
in the center of the room against a pile of robes.

"I've come back, Nahlekadeya," he said solemnly,
and her tiny eyes almost disappeared as she smiled a
toothless grin.

"And you have brought the woman," she said, nodding to Brittany, who knelt down too, resting on her
heels. She knew that Apache custom did not allow

women to sit cross-legged before the occupants of the tepee they visited. "Blake has told me you wish to know about Rubia," the old woman continued, addressing Brittany.

Her eyebrows shot up in surprise. "Rubia" had been Elizabeth's name in the camp. Surely this woman wouldn't have known her. Brittany looked at Blake questioningly.

"Nahledkadeya is one hundred and three summers old," he told her. "Why don't you ask her?"

Brittany turned toward the old woman, whose face was a mask of wrinkles.

"Did you know Rubia?" she asked.

"As a very little girl, yes. I knew them all—Cochise, Nachise, the life in the hills when we were as free as the birds. Rubia was like a wild doe, frightened of every noise in the forest at first. The women grew to love her. She was kind and good and never complained, no matter how quickly we had to move, for the whites were clever in tracking us. Rubia was a good Indian and it made Nachise's heart heavy when he had to send her back to her people."

"Why did he send her back?" Brittany asked. "She would have stayed if he'd let her."

The answer was slow in coming and Brittany thought that perhaps the woman had not heard her. Then the husky voice said, "The treaty forced him. He could not jeopardize the peace his father had brought for his people by following his heart's desire. Nachise was almost as noble as his father." The old woman's small, dark eyes shone as memories returned to her from across the sea of time.

Blake and Brittany spent the afternoon in Nahlekadeya's company, listening until she grew too tired to talk. Finally she signaled an end to the meeting. They thanked the old woman and left her to rest.

Blake was silent until they were some distance from

the tepee. "Did she answer your remaining question?" he asked.

"Yes, yes, she did. How did you know about her?" Brittany asked eagerly.

"I told you, I've been here before. I was curious about Elizabeth myself and thought there might be someone here who had heard stories about her. I didn't expect to find anyone alive who had actually known her." They arrived at where their horses were tied.

"I think your act is a big humbug, Blake Kincade, this 'live for now' facade. You're as interested in the past as I am."

"It's not a facade and, yes, I am interested in the past. But not interested enough to let today go by without living it too." His words annoyed her, but before she had a chance to say anything else in refutation, he added, "The L.A. Grand National is in two days. It means the end of the racing season for me. I want you to be there."

"To see you possibly hurt? No, thank you, Blake," she said firmly. "I can't stop you, but I don't have to watch." How could he race again, risking everything, after what had happened between them last night?

He shrugged his shoulders, pretending it didn't matter to him. "Suit yourself. Live in your shell, Brittany. It's your shell. Now you'd better get ready. I've got to get back in time to see that the race car's transported up to Riverside."

Brittany was tempted to inform him haughtily that she intended to stay at the reservation a few more days, but this time, unlike with Peter, she decided against it. She wanted to be with him for as long as possible. "Alright, I'll come back with you," she agreed.

"Thank you for the favor," he muttered moodily. She said nothing more and they remounted and headed their horses back to the hotel.

That afternoon they seemed to fly home, making record time. Blake appeared to be taking out his frustration

on the car, and he took sharp turns that would have sent
Brittany sprawling against him but for her seat belt. She
kept silent as well, not knowing how to break the wall
Blake had locked around himself. She began to wonder
once again if he cared about her at all. If he did, why
did he insist on risking his life in the race? But then,
even if she. didn't come there would be another woman
to take her place and cheer him on.

Suddenly she felt a pang in her heart. She didn't want
another woman to take her place. She wanted to tell
Blake she had changed her mind, but she couldn't find
the words. Doing so would mean admitting once again
that she loved him. And the last thing she wanted was
to burden him with her love when he had never said he
felt the same for her.

"Britt, I need a favor."

Brittany turned from the letter she was writing at her
desk, surprised to see Ambroise enter her room, even
more surprised at his asking her a favor.

"Blake wants me to fly up to watch him race," Ambroise continued, pulling his chair alongside hers. "I
don't like these races of Blake's, as you well know.
They're senseless and show a total disregard for life and
limb. But Blake's never asked me to come before. I can't
say no—and I won't go by myself."

"Etienne—" she began to suggest.

"Will be indisposed," he interrupted cryptically.

"But the journal—"

"I'm more than satisfied with your efforts and I refuse
to be accused of working you to death. Besides," he
added with a twinkle in his eye, "I'm your boss."

She bit her lip, then smiled. "Well, I won't stand in
the way of a reconciliation, if it amounts to that."

"It amounts to that," he told her, patting her hand.
"Good girl, Britt. The jet will take us there in the morning."

"The jet?" she echoed. Was there no end to the Kincade money?

"Yes. I'm having the captain take us in the Lear jet. There will be a few local reporters flying up as well. After all, Blake's a celebrity around here." A note of pride had crept into his voice.

Brittany nodded. Ambroise made hiring a Lear jet sound so simple that she couldn't help but smile.

"Some of Blake's friends are coming also."

"Is Sheila?" she asked without thinking.

Ambroise shrugged his shoulders. "Possibly. I just know about Molly and her husband. See you later, Britt. Knew I could count on you."

Brittany chose her best dress to wear to the race. She wasn't about to stand around looking drab in comparison to the other women who were bound to come along for the event. Actually she was thinking of Sheila. And with good reason, it turned out.

She heard the car pull up that evening before dinner and, looking out her bedroom window, she saw Sheila emerge. Her chauffeur left with the car after he had walked Sheila to the front door with her overnight case.

Brittany hurried to the top of the stairs, keeping to one side so as not to be seen. She heard Sheila announce her own presence and call out for Blake when the butler informed her he wasn't sure if Master Blake was in.

Blake appeared in the doorway of the den, looking more than a little annoyed. From where she stood, Brittany could see that he'd been watching tapes of past car races on the giant viewing screeen. Both Johnny and Molly were standing in the background.

"What are you doing here?" Blake asked Sheila. His voice was a little tight, despite his easy manner. A glass of wine was still in his hand. "I thought we agreed—"

Sheila slipped the glass from him and took a long sip, then pressed her lips against his, stopping his question.

"I've come to spend the night and hold your hand before the big race. I'll make all your fears go away," she added, running her hand through his hair.

"I'm not afraid, Sheila," he told her, pulling away.

"Ah, Blake the fearless, then. Good, you can make some of mine go away then, like the fear that I'm being dumped." Her lips formed a hard red line. "Now do you ask me to stay nicely, or do I have to make a great big scene?" Her smile was icy. "I'm very good at making scenes," she promised.

Molly joined them just then. "Sheila," she said, "Blake was just showing us his tapes of old races. Why don't you come in and watch with us? It's almost like really being there yourself." She ushered the blond woman into the other room.

Blake's expression was somber. "Penworth," he called to the butler, "take this case to the blue room. Sheila will be staying the night."

Brittany felt a stab of pain as she returned to her room.

Dinner that evening was an ordeal. Molly did her best to keep up a light conversation among Ambroise, her husband, and Brittany. Her efforts to draw Sheila out met with little success. Sheila had eyes only for Blake and she monopolized his attention.

"Blake, did I tell you Britt's agreed to accompany me to the race?" Ambroise asked his son, eyeing Sheila rather caustically.

Blake turned surprised eyes to Brittany, who looked past him, not trusting herself to meet his blue eyes. He'd see her hurt, and she didn't want his pity.

"I'm riding with you up front," Sheila told Blake.

"Sheila, I already tried to explain to you that there's no room," Blake said in an even tone.

"Then bump the excess baggage," she replied through clenched teeth, tossing her head in Brittany's direction.

"Young woman, you will keep a civil tongue in your

head at my table," Ambroise told her, his voice growing loud with impatience.

Sheila fell momentarily silent at his rebuke, then turned to Blake with an ultimatum in her eyes. "Then I ride in your lap," she decided. "It'll be cozier."

Molly interrupted. "One of the reporters can be prevailed upon to stay behind, or at least give up his seat, Blake," she said, effectively tabling the discussion.

Sheila glared triumphantly at Brittany, who kept her growing hostility to herself. If Blake couldn't put Sheila in her place, or tell her to stay home, that was his choice. She tried to tell herself it didn't matter. But it did. Very much.

At dawn the next morning members of the Kincade household, as well as guests and reporters, hurried to and fro in an effort to get ready to leave on time. Brittany rode with Ambroise in the Rolls-Royce. She noted that Sheila had plunked herself in Blake's car and sat waiting for him to show up. She waved gaily at Brittany as the Rolls sped away.

"I cannot stomach that girl," Ambroise said, staring straight ahead. "Blake certainly has exhibited his share of poor choice in women."

Brittany leaned back in her seat, hurt by his comment. "It looks like he still does," she said under her breath, referring to Sheila.

The old man patted her hand. "No, I've found his taste has improved a great deal of late." Brittany said nothing, wishing that Ambroise's words were true, that she really was Blake's choice in a woman.

All the way to the airport Brittany envisioned Sheila's thigh rubbing against Blake's, Sheila's hand touching him, teasing him into wanting her again. And Sheila wasn't hard to get, Brittany reflected bitterly. Blake would have all he could handle with her. She tried not to consider how little their one night together must have meant to him. Otherwise he would have sought her out, wouldn't he?

The flight to Riverside was no less uncomfortable. Blake was surrounded by reporters and practically smothered by Sheila. Brittany shared a seat with Ambroise, who kept her occupied in a conversation she only half heard. Molly joined them later in an obvious effort to cheer Brittany up, but the younger woman found it difficult to respond with more than polite answers. She kept hearing Sheila's breathy laughter and the reporters' enthusiastic guffaws.

Several times Blake turned toward the back of the plane to try and get Brittany's attention, but she turned her face away, not wanting him to see her unhappiness. She felt too hurt to confront him, to demand that he account for his actions and clarify his feelings for her. She was too afraid to hear words that she felt certain would break her heart.

They landed shortly and disembarked quickly. Blake rushed off to check on his car and Sheila disappeared with him, followed by a trail of reporters.

"Ah, now we can finally breathe," Ambroise told Brittany. The pilot helped Ambroise into his wheelchair and guided him down the special ramp, Molly and Johnny following behind him.

"Where do we go from here?" Brittany asked, not knowing anything about the area.

"I have a car waiting for us. Ah, there it is," Ambroise said, spotting the waiting chauffeur. He turned in his seat. "Molly, would you and your husband care for a lift?"

Molly smiled, her round face lighting up. "Thank you, Ambroise. We'd love to take you up on the offer."

The four of them got into the car and the chauffeur waited for his instructions.

"We do have plenty of time, so if anyone wishes to make a stop at the suite of rooms I've rented for us before the race," Ambroise suggested. But no one did. "Alright, Andrews, to the International Raceway," he instructed.

Within an hour they had settled down in the stands. Brittany watched forty-two cars line up. Blake's silver racing car was in row three. For six straight hours her eyes hardly left it. She couldn't believe the speeds the cars maintained, flying by at an average of one hundred and eighty miles per hour.

For the most part the race was uneventful—until the last hour. Despite her resolve not to care, Brittany felt herself growing more and more tense as time passed. What if Blake were hurt? It didn't happen often, but sometimes drivers were even killed. What if having Sheila around ruined his concentration? A driver had to be aware of nothing but his car and the road. Distractions could be deadly. And what about his car? The sleek racer had been checked and rechecked, but there was always room for human error. What if . . .

"It'll be alright, honey," Molly said, patting Brittany's ice-cold hand. "I've been through this myself and I know what you're feeling. Every time Johnny raced, my heart was in my throat."

Brittany nodded, hardly hearing.

The officials called penalties and pulled several cars out of the race. Other cars pulled into their pits to be checked and refueled. Brittany's knuckles turned white with tension. Her excitement mounted as the cars became fewer in number. Blake's car was in third place, hugging the embankment as it flew on, pushing to be first.

Brittany's heart seemed to stop beating altogether as she watched him swerve to avoid a car that had spun out of control after losing its rear axle. It collided with three other cars, sending two of them into one another. One burst into flames and suddenly men were running from the pits with fire extinguishers. Miraculously no one was hurt. The flag went out and the cars pulled into their pits to refuel while the track was cleared. Within minutes they were speeding around the track once again.

Another car suddenly leaked oil and sent the car directly behind it crashing into the railing. And still it went on, with death a hairbreadth away, and the trophy getting closer every second.

"Ladies and gentlemen, Andre Pierceoff's 4.9 Ferrari has dropped out of the race!" the announcer cried. Moans and cheers rose across the stands. "And it looks like Gilles Bertram is going to be the winner," said the same voice over the loudspeaker. "No, wait, wait, Blake Kincade is making the most fantastic last-ditch effort I've ever seen. His car has wings!"

Please, please let him be alright, Brittany prayed, straining her eyes to see the silver streak.

"He's gaining! He's gaining! Ladies and gentlemen, he has passed Gilles Bertram's Maserati! Nothing can stop him now!"

The silver dart flew past the madly waving flag. Blake had won!

The roar of the crowd was deafening. A new victor had emerged. Blake climbed out of his car and leaned against the top as he took off his helmet. His face was smudged with dirt, but he was a resplendent victor. Photographers ran out of the stands, snapping their cameras. A trophy appeared magically in Blake's hand. Suddenly he was surrounded by women who were kissing him and clinging to his arms. Champagne was being poured into the winner's cup. And through it all Sheila stood next to him, turning her face toward the photographers.

Despite the hoopla, the look on Blake's face was not triumphant, not the face of a man who had won a grueling six-hour race, missing disaster by inches. Every once in a while his eyes scanned the crowd. But Brittany dared not let herself think he was looking for her.

She watched the whole event, her throat dry, her eyes

stinging with unshed tears. Blake was being taken off to the winner's circle and being swallowed up by a sea of reporters, well-wishers, and adoring women.

"Let's go back to the hotel," Molly was shouting to Brittany above the noise. "We'd better rest up for the victory party."

Brittany nodded, not really hearing the words, not really caring. She helped guide Ambroise's wheelchair safely through the thinning crowd. She looked back only once and saw the characteristic devil-may-care smile back on Blake's lips as he draped his arm around two shapely women. Brittany wondered briefly what had happened to Sheila.

"We can stay if you want to," Ambroise was saying to her.

"No, I don't want to," she replied. She climbed into the Rolls-Royce and stared blindly out the window.

chapter

11

THE PARTY WAS LOUD. Brittany could hear it all the way down the hall in her room. Ambroise and then Johnny and Molly had tried to talk her into going, but she had refused, begging off with the time-worn excuse of a headache. She couldn't explain that it was her heart that hurt. After all, she had known from the first that she would eventually be replaced by other women in Blake's life. She had no reason to feel upset now, seeing him being kissed and hugged and thinking that arms other than hers would embrace him later that night. Yet the very thought brought fresh pain to her already ravaged heart.

She went to bed early and tossed and turned for hours, finally falling into a fitful sleep. Sometime during the night she thought she heard someone knocking on her door, but she didn't wake up enough to answer, and the next day she was sure it had been a dream.

During the flight home the next day the reporters on board took up all of Blake's time, which was just as well, Brittany decided. His preoccupation prevented her from going up to him to tell him good-bye. She was afraid that if she said the words, she might never undertake the action.

Only once did she wonder why Sheila wasn't on the plane.

Brittany fingered the brittle pages of Elizabeth's journal, which were lying on her lap, as if taking strength from them. Elizabeth had gone back to her old world, leaving behind the man she loved. Brittany would have to do the same.

As soon as they arrived at the house and said a few words of farewell to the people in the car, Brittany headed for her room. Ambroise looked after her, puzzled.

"How was the race?" Etienne asked her as she passed him in the hall.

"Blake won," she answered, fighting back sudden tears.

Once in her room she took her suitcase down from the closet shelf and began to pack. She gazed fondly at the clothes Ambroise had bought for her. She couldn't take them. They belonged to this world. As of tomorrow she would be a single working girl again. Thank goodness Peter Dane had come along when he had.

Carefully she folded the four dresses she had originally brought with her, then put on the two-piece brown suit she had worn the first day. She combed her hair back. She was about to put it into a bun when there was a knock on the door.

"I'm busy," she said, thinking it might be Blake and not about to let him in.

"Then I'll wait," came the reply. It was Ambroise.

She opened the door. "I'm sorry, Mr. Kincade," she apologized, "I didn't know it was you." She held the door open wide for him.

He propelled his chair into the room, then studied her shrewdly. "So the butterfly is returning to her cocoon, is that it?"

"I'm very sorry I won't be able to finish your book for you. At least not here. I can't stay here any longer."

"So you're going to run away," he accused her.

"I am not running away," she retorted, her pride piqued.

"What do you call that?" he asked, jerking his hand at her suitcase.

"Being sensible," she replied.

"Being a coward, in my book. Haven't you learned anything from my great-grandmother? She had the courage to face up to her situation and to fight to survive. She didn't withdraw and die when life got tough."

"I'm not about to die, but I won't chase after a man who doesn't love me," she said firmly.

"Chase a man? From what I can see, Blake's the one doing all the chasing. And that's never happened to him before. He's always had to fight women off. Every time I turned around he was taking you off somewhere. I don't recall you taking him anywhere."

"Mr. Kincade, your son only wants one thing from me," Brittany said, turning away, too embarrassed to admit that she had already given Blake what he wanted and it obviously hadn't been enough.

"Then you're a poor judge of character, Britt," Ambroise told her. "Of course he wants that 'thing.' You're a very attractive woman, with some help from my wardrobe," he added, frowning at the suit she was wearing. "And he's a man. He'd be a fool not to want to bed you. But that's not all there is. I know my son, for all the arguments between us. If you want him, dig in and fight for him. Princes don't fall in your lap the way they do in fairy tales, Britt. This is the real world, after all."

"I thought you didn't like pushy women," she answered, referring to his words when they first met. But her eyes were twinkling now and the hopelessness that had made her hands so slow at packing was completely blown away.

"In your case, I'll make an exception," Ambroise told her. "You were a very confident young woman when you came here, but you had never had to meet a single real challenge. Prove to me I wasn't wrong about you."

"Alright, I will," she said, a smile coming over her

face. She kissed his cheek impulsively.

"And for heaven's sake, burn those clothes, will you?" he said, as he left the room. "He's downstairs in the living room," he said by way of parting.

Brittany quickly shed her ugly brown suit and took a striking blue dress out of the closet. She touched the thin straps and smiled, remembering how he liked to slip them off her shoulders. Well, she was wearing this one just for him. It had a slit up the right thigh, fit snugly about her hips, and dipped low in front. She refreshened her makeup and checked herself in the mirror. Was that really her? she wondered. And then she went downstairs to confront him, to find out once and for all exactly what he felt for her, what he wanted from their relationship. His words might devastate her and make her have to leave, but at least she would know one way or the other. At least she would have confronted him instead of running away.

As she passed the den, Ambroise gave her the high sign. She nodded and opened the double doors leading into the living room.

Blake was there, still surrounded by reporters, each intent on getting an exclusive scoop. A local hero made good press. Again Brittany noticed that Sheila was missing.

Blake saw Brittany enter the room and stopped in mid-sentence. After an initial surprise, the expression on his face grew hard. "Gentleman, that'll be all for now," he announced. "You have your story and I'll be more than happy to see you later if there are further questions. But right now I have a personal matter to attend to." He boldly ushered them toward the door, refusing to say any more. He closed the door behind them and turned toward Brittany. His blue eyes were smoldering with anger.

"Where were you?" he demanded.

She was thrown off balance. "When?"

"At the race!"

"I didn't think you'd even noticed I was gone. Sheila was clinging to you so hard I was sure she'd stop your circulation."

"Yes, she was with me then, but she's not going to be anymore. You don't understand about Sheila."

"I understand all too well," Brittany retorted, angry at herself as much as at him. This wasn't going at all the way she wanted it to.

Blake gripped her shoulder. One strap slipped down but he didn't notice. "No, you don't understand," he insisted. "Sheila can be a hysterical woman and I couldn't find a way of getting rid of her without causing a scene. Fortunately her love of money far outweighed her attachment to me." A self-satisfied smile came to his lips. "I introduced her to the guy who came in second in the race. He's a Frenchman and owns a chateau on the Riviera. The last time I saw Sheila she was on his arm." He paused. "Now do you believe me when I say I'm not interested in Sheila? I haven't been interested in her for a long, long time."

"Well, if you've accomplished what you set out to do, why are you so angry?" Brittany asked, still not sure of him.

"I'm angry, you idiot, because at the high point of my life you left me with a hollow victory. It didn't mean anything without you there to share it. I wanted you in that winner's circle with me, not Sheila. And where were you at the party?"

"I didn't go."

"I know that. But you weren't in your room either."

"So it *was* you who knocked?" she asked. Her heart was beating fast and hard. He had actually come looking for her!

"Oh, you *were* in your room, then, playing hard to get, as usual."

She pulled away from him. "I don't play hard to get. I just want a relationship where I'm not part of a crowd."

Blake looked sternly down at her. "Damn your hide, Brittany. Ever since you came into this house you've filled my mind and my senses. You've made me want to do noble, crazy things like tearing up my little black book." She began to smile. "And then you came to my hotel room the other night," he continued. "You looked so damn vulnerable and brave. Why did you come to me if you didn't think I wanted you, that I loved you?"

"I knew you *wanted* me," she explained, "but I didn't think you loved me. I just knew I had to show you how much I loved *you*. But afterward you acted as if nothing had changed between us, and for me everything had changed. I was afraid to ask what I meant to you. And then Sheila showed up and all those other women..." Her voice trailed off.

"Oh, Brittany, Brittany," he scolded her softly. "Do I have to get down on one knee to convince you?"

"Do you mean get down to pick up the pieces of your little black book?" she asked, confused.

"No, to ask you to marry me!"

His words took her breath away. She couldn't believe he meant them. She had loved him for so long, but never once had she dared to hope he would ever love her enough to make the kind of commitment she longed to make to him. She stared at him, stupefied, and he chuckled deeply.

"Did you hear me, Brittany?" he said softly. "I asked you to marry me."

She shook her head in disbelief. Suddenly she had to know one thing. "Is it because I look like Anne?" she asked shyly.

"Anne was a special person, but you're someone entirely different," he told her. Then he took her into his arms and this time she didn't hesitate. She felt as if she had finally come home. "I love you and I don't want to lose you when this project of my father's is over," he said. "Marry me, Brittany, marry me or I swear you'll have no peace from me. I don't want to hear the word 'no' out of your mouth ever again."

Her green eyes shone as her sensuous mouth curved upward. "Oh, Blake," she whispered. "Yes, yes, yes."

"That's much better," he said just before his mouth covered hers, sending flaming arrows of joy throughout her body.

He swept her up into his arms and began to walk toward the stairs. As they passed the den the door slowly closed.

"Good old dad," Blake chuckled under his breath.

It was as if they were utterly alone in the house, alone with their passion and their love for one another. Blake carried Brittany into his room and shut the door behind them with a nudge of his elbow.

"You're going to be mine forever," he vowed, setting her down next to the bed. Brittany put her arms about his neck.

"Prove it," she said.

His lips found hers and the passion that erupted between them was even greater than the first time. Blake slipped off her clothes almost without her noticing, his warm hands caressing her over and over again, reducing her to quivering anticipation and drawing her near, as suddenly there was nothing between their naked bodies.

Brittany sank into the soft comforter on Blake's bed, pulling him along with her, her senses filled with the scent and feel of his maleness. His body covered hers, demanding, urgent, yet holding back, as if savoring every golden moment that passed between them. His dark head lowered as his mouth forged a path of fire that covered all of her, causing her heart to hammer almost painfully in her breast. Her breath grew ragged as his hands, caressing her thighs, gave way to his lips. Swirling heat was everywhere as she clung to him, caressing him with a rhythm that he matched with his own powerful strokes.

The world he opened again for her was like none that

had existed before in any realm of her imagination. Overwhelming excitement, the pulsating joy of anticipation, took hold of her as he made her his again.

And then, as they descended from paradise together, she saw his mischievous eyes peering into her face. "I hope the future Mrs. Kincade is prepared for many moments like this," he said in a whisper that tickled her cheek.

"More prepared than you'll ever know," Brittany said, reaching for him again.

As their lips met in a kiss that was sweet with the promise of passion and tender with the fulfillment of trust, Brittany felt that she had neither entered Blake's world nor brought him into hers. They were creating a world of their own, forging a new life together from the smoldering embers of a desire that had burst into glorious life.

WATCH FOR
6 NEW TITLES EVERY MONTH!

Second Chance at Love™

____ 05703-7 **FLAMENCO NIGHTS #1** Susanna Collins

____ 05637-5 **WINTER LOVE SONG #2** Meredith Kingston

____ 05624-3 **THE CHADBOURNE LUCK #3** Lucia Curzon

____ 05777-0 **OUT OF A DREAM #4** Jennifer Rose

____ 05878-5 **GLITTER GIRL #5** Jocelyn Day

____ 05863-7 **AN ARTFUL LADY #6** Sabina Clark

____ 05694-4 **EMERALD BAY #7** Winter Ames

____ 05776-2 **RAPTURE REGAINED #8** Serena Alexander

____ 05801-7 **THE CAUTIOUS HEART #9** Philippa Heywood

____ 05907-2 **ALOHA YESTERDAY #10** Meredith Kingston

____ 05638-3 **MOONFIRE MELODY #11** Lily Bradford

____ 06132-8 **MEETING WITH THE PAST #12** Caroline Halter

____ 05623-5 **WINDS OF MORNING #13** Laurie Marath

____ 05704-5 **HARD TO HANDLE #14** Susanna Collins

____ 06067-4 **BELOVED PIRATE #15** Margie Michaels

____ 05978-1 **PASSION'S FLIGHT #16** Marilyn Mathieu

____ 05847-5 **HEART OF THE GLEN #17** Lily Bradford

____ 05977-3 **BIRD OF PARADISE #18** Winter Ames

____ 05705-3 **DESTINY'S SPELL #19** Susanna Collins

____ 06106-9 **GENTLE TORMENT #20** Johanna Phillips

____ 06059-3 **MAYAN ENCHANTMENT #21** Lila Ford

____ 06301-0 **LED INTO SUNLIGHT #22** Claire Evans

____ 06131-X **CRYSTAL FIRE #23** Valerie Nye

____ 06150-6 **PASSION'S GAMES #24** Meredith Kingston

____ 06160-3 **GIFT OF ORCHIDS #25** Patti Moore

____ 06108-5 **SILKEN CARESSES #26** Samantha Carroll

WHAT READERS SAY ABOUT
SECOND CHANCE AT LOVE